LAST SWORD IN
THE WEST

RYAN KIRK

Copyright 2020 by Waterstone Media

All rights reserved.

No part of this book may be reproduced in any form or by any electronic
or mechanical means, including information storage and retrieval systems,
without permission from the author, except for the use of brief
quotations.

WATERSTONE
MEDIA

For Mike

1

A cold wind snapped through the tall grass, and Tomas glanced behind him as though worried the ghosts of his past had finally caught him.

No spectral shadows pursued him this night, though. Tolkin set on the western horizon as Shen rose in the east, the dual moons casting plenty of light. The grasses surrounding him stood tall enough to hide an army, but armies rarely traveled this far west. He saw no one, living or dead, for as far as his sight could carry.

Tomas kept his arms folded across his chest inside his robes. The wind stole the warmth from his body when it gusted. He felt Elzeth stir, but did not wake him. The night wasn't that cold.

The trail he followed barely deserved the title. It had once been used by local game, perhaps, but not recently. And there wasn't a single footprint to be found. He wouldn't have been surprised to find his feet were the first human ones on the trail.

Just as he desired.

But even out here, humans marched relentlessly west. A sliver of Tolkin was still visible on the horizon when Tomas came across the road.

It was little more than two rutted wheel tracks, but Tomas growled quietly at them anyway. He looked east, where the carts had all come from, and he clenched one of the long daggers hidden underneath his robes.

His anger wakened Elzeth. "Haven't seen any sign of others for three days," he said.

"Not long enough," Tomas replied.

"Going to follow it?"

Tomas looked to the west. It was the same direction he meant to travel. The game trail hadn't been much more than a passing hope, a vague dream of roasted meat. But prey around here was either scarce, or better at avoiding him than he was at finding it.

His stomach rumbled at the thought of a full meal.

He followed the road west. Where there were humans, there was food.

Only a few miles later the road split in two. One set of ruts turned slightly to the north. The others went straight west. Tomas bent down and felt each set with his hand. Most travelers apparently preferred the path that led west.

No sign or marker gave him any further guidance. He found a stick on the ground and tossed it in the air. It spun lazily over his head, then landed, pointing roughly north. Tomas took the road that turned that direction.

"Really?" Elzeth asked.

Tomas shrugged, and Elzeth fell silent.

He found his destination sooner than he expected. Shen hadn't even reached its zenith when he spotted the flickering lights of a watchtower off in the distance. Elzeth stirred again, and Tomas' eyes sharpened.

There wasn't one watchtower, but two. The closer of the two almost blocked Tomas' line of sight to the second. He frowned as he looked around. One tower was unusual enough in these parts. He'd never heard of a town with two. Both had watchers within.

Elzeth rumbled.

"What do you think?" Tomas asked.

"Your sword still sharp?"

Tomas grunted. He felt the same. But the idea of a warm meal proved a temptation too great. He continued on.

He heard the town not much later. It sounded like a celebration, like the town knew just how unlikely their continued survival was, and they shouted their defiance to any who dared come close.

Or, Tomas thought as he approached, everyone was simply raging drunk.

The sounds brought a hint of a smile to his face. Once, this town might have been his kind of place. Perhaps someday, it would be again. A place where he could happily disappear into a crowd of faceless revelers.

Despite the din from the town, Tomas heard her before he saw her. The tall grasses and softly rolling hills hid her until he was almost next to her.

He slowed but didn't stop.

There was no mistaking the sound of a mother weeping.

He'd heard it plenty.

Tomas stopped beside a fence, short enough to easily step over. Straight lines of grave markers proclaimed the purpose of the small plot of land. The markers were in the style of the old faith, a simple square post, the deceased's name and age at death inscribed in the wood. There were quite a few markers for a town this far west.

A man and a woman knelt next to one of the graves. The

dirt of the grave was dark and loose. Quite a few of the plots nearby looked new, too. The wild grasses hadn't even had time to grow on most.

Though Tomas stood a dozen paces from the grieving couple, he could read the name and age of the dead. Their son, he assumed, had been young. He watched in silence for several long moments, feeling like an intruder on an intimate scene. The couple was so wrapped up in their grief they didn't even notice him.

Tomas wavered.

A particularly strong breeze arose, and Tomas' cloak snapped in the wind.

The man's head twisted rapidly at the sound. He took a step back at the sight of Tomas, but Tomas held up his hands in a gesture of peace. The woman made no motion at all. Grief had become her whole world.

His presence noticed, Tomas stepped over the fence into the cemetery. Entering the grounds by any means except the gate was considered a sin by the faithful, but Tomas had long since stopped caring about their opinion.

The grieving man looked torn between anger and fear. In a few moments, one would take over, but Tomas paid him little mind. Moving deliberately, so as not to further frighten the man into rash action, Tomas reached into a pocket of his cloak to pull out a small bottle.

He stopped beside the grave, and the mother's eyes saw him for the first time. Before she could react, he pulled the stopper from the bottle and took a sip.

The fine wine was a blessing for his dry lips and throat. The vintage was one of the best he'd ever tasted. Complex layers of flavor coated his tongue, and for a moment, he hesitated. The wine was likely worth several times whatever this couple made in a year.

And it was really good.

He took one more sip, savoring the experience, relishing the pleasure the wine gave him.

Then he took the rest of the bottle and poured it on their boy's grave marker. "No one should pass without having tasted a fine wine," he said.

When they realized what he had done, both parents bowed deeply to him. When the mother rose, she reached out to clasp his hand. Her grip was cold as ice, and Tomas let his hand warm hers. Tears streamed down her face, and although she couldn't bring herself to speak, she nodded to him.

Tomas returned the gesture and let her hands drop.

When he raised his eyes, he met the hard glare of the father. The older man's gaze traveled down to the sword at Tomas' side, then back up.

"You another mercenary?" he asked, the word a curse.

Tomas shook his head.

The man laughed, the sound bitter and harsh. "You will be soon, if you're going into town."

Tomas glanced that way, the town barely visible from where he stood. Only the dual watchtowers served as obvious landmarks.

He turned to leave the couple to their grief. But he had loosened something in the father.

"A tough man, eh?" The insult was practically shouted, and Tomas winced against the disregard to the dead. "My boy was strong, too. One of the best swords in town. Ask anyone. Didn't matter one bit, though. Not with a dagger in his back. And it's all because of you and your lot. I hope your soul burns!"

The man collapsed, his grief-fueled anger spent.

Tomas nodded, then left the cemetery.

He didn't know if the father's last words to him were meant to be heard or not. Tomas didn't turn to see, and they were spoken softly.

"You better know how to use that sword, son. If you die a stranger in this town, no one will dig you a grave."

2

The night was well on by the time Tomas stepped foot in town, but no one looked bound for their beds anytime soon. Brightly lit saloons and crowded gambling halls competed to decide whose customers were the loudest. A pair of drunk young men supported one another on a journey from one saloon to the next. Their attention, limited as it was, was so focused on the completion of their quest they didn't even notice him.

The town felt a bit larger now that he was within its limits. The heart of the town was this street, cutting as straight as an arrow through the town's center. All the businesses, Tomas figured, would be on this street, with the private homes tucked behind.

As new arrivals would come from the east, they would build even farther away from the main street. The town would grow, continuing its relentless advance against the wild prairie. If it was successful, someday it would become a proper city. He'd seen the same process repeated in dozens of similar towns. The story was always the same, told over and over across the west.

Hopefully the food here was worth it.

Tomas paused less than a third of the way down the street, next to the first of the watchtowers. The second was at the other end of town, where there was very little activity. Both towers still had people within, but Tomas saw the watchers' attention wasn't on the harsh wilds, but on the town below.

Elzeth was now fully awake. "Odd."

Tomas grunted his agreement.

A pair stepped out into the street before him. A young man and woman, their proximity to one another more than implying their relationship. The man walked with a confident swagger, the master of his own tiny domain. The sword at his side was too big for him.

"Welcome, stranger," the man said.

Tomas offered the man the slightest of bows, then tipped his conical straw hat to the woman. "Greetings, ma'am."

The girl giggled. "I like him."

The young man tensed. Not much, and he relaxed less than a second later, but Tomas noticed. Unsurprisingly, the boy lacked the necessary control to master the weapon he carried.

Most did.

The overly confident warrior stepped to within three feet of Tomas, puffed out his chest, and glared at Tomas' own sword. "You even know how to use that?"

Elzeth laughed.

Tomas kept his face straight. "I'm still learning."

The young man took another step forward. He stood a few inches taller than Tomas and sought to make the most out of the perceived advantage. He sneered. "Well, if you think you're any good, the boss is always looking for true warriors. It's dangerous work, but the gold is good, and you won't find a more entertaining town in the whole land."

"Just passing through."

The man laughed. "Probably for the best. You look like you're as likely to cut yourself as your target. But if you change your mind, tell the boss Eiro sent you. My name will at least get you an audience."

Tomas gave Eiro another slight bow, then let him take the girl's arm and continue on. Eiro looked as if he was on patrol. Why, Tomas couldn't begin to guess. But out of the corner of his eye he saw the girl turn and give him one long, appraising look. Then her eyes locked on his, and a slow smile spread across her face.

"I like him," Elzeth said.

The corner of Tomas' lips turned up in a grin, a gesture the woman certainly appeared to misunderstand.

"Sure you do. Now let's find some food."

They walked farther down the street. Most places remained open despite the lateness of the hour. From the sounds of revelry emanating from them, it was no surprise they chose to serve guests at such times. It sounded as though rivers of gold were flowing through the town. Which was also odd, as Tomas was sure this place was too small and too new to even show up on the maps out east.

The town reminded him of himself as a younger man. Loud and brash, certain he was bigger and more important than he actually was.

He felt no desire to partake in the rambunctious behavior that surrounded him this night. His meetings, both with Eiro and the mourning couple, had left a sour taste in the back of his mouth. He passed the bustling gambling halls and saloons and soon he'd put the noise behind him.

Tomas walked the same street, but it might as well have

been in a different town. Ahead, the last third of the town was nearly silent. Most shops were closed, and the only people to be seen were two pairs of uniformed guards patrolling the streets.

Elzeth bristled at the sight of the uniforms. Tomas felt power rush through his veins. His vision sharpened until the details almost overwhelmed him. The miles he'd trekked already today fell off him like dust knocked off boots.

"Easy," Tomas said.

One pair of guards approached. Their uniforms were white, to remind the world of their purity. Three wavy lines over their hearts were the symbol of their faith. The lines were sewn into the uniforms with red thread. According to the book, red symbolized their willingness to shed their blood for their faith. In Tomas' experience, the red thread meant it was far more likely the blood of an innocent would soon be spilled.

Knights of the First Church of Holy Water.

Only the strength of his will kept his hand away from his sword.

"Greetings, stranger," the one on Tomas' right said. "Do you have need of food, or a place to lay your head tonight?"

The knight was tall with short dark hair. Every word he spoke grated against Tomas' ears. No doubt, the knight would call his offer hospitality, and would believe the claim with his whole heart. But there was a gleam in his eye, an eagerness Tomas shied away from. What the knight really saw was an opportunity to save another soul.

But what were knights doing out here? Perhaps the town had a mission. That, he understood. But knights were well-trained and expensive to keep around. The young man before him was probably as dangerous as a dozen Eiros, and probably cost about that much, too. The church didn't send knights unless someone needed killing.

"This is what you get for following the directions of a stick," Elzeth grumbled.

"I'd rather not spend the night in a mission," Tomas said. "No disrespect intended."

The knight didn't miss a beat. "Then you're in luck. We have a mission and a rest."

"What in the three hells have you walked us into?" Elzeth asked.

"I've never heard of a rest this far west," Tomas said. And that was true. Up until a few moments ago, he would have said the last rest was hundreds of miles east of here.

The knight's partner, a woman with light hair, took a slow step to the side. The movement didn't draw much attention to itself, but it gave her the space to clear her sword and attack Tomas without endangering her partner. She'd heard the hesitation in his voice.

Tomas swore to himself.

He really didn't want to fight two knights.

Judging from their stances, he would need Elzeth's help.

And then he would have to run again.

He was tired of running.

He fixed the girl with a stare. It let her know that he had noticed her movement, and that it didn't frighten him. Let her wonder on that for a while. She could debate whether he was that good or that mad.

The first knight watched the entire exchange. His smile remained fixed. He appeared as confident as Tomas felt. Though he made no move, Tomas recognized the knight's stance. His sword could be in hand in a heartbeat.

Tomas' blood boiled. His vision was so sharp it hurt, and

the distant sounds of the drunks behind him thundered in his ears. He wanted these knights to try him.

"It's a new rest," the first knight said, "so it's no surprise you haven't heard of it. It's the farthest west we've built so far. And you're more than welcome. We'd be honored to have you as our guest."

In other words, he wasn't being given a choice.

Which, had the knight known Tomas at all, was the worst mistake he could have made.

"No thanks," Tomas said, barely managing to remain polite. He turned on his heel, making one last attempt at avoiding bloodshed.

A moment later, he heard the unmistakable sound of a sword being drawn.

3

An individual life was rarely as resilient as most people liked to believe. Death quietly terrified everyone, and most dealt with the existential fear by pretending the threat wasn't that serious. In a previous life, Tomas had known plenty of young men and women who believed they would live forever, despite the abundant evidence to the contrary.

They had all lived hard back then, their bodies overflowing both with ale and confidence. Tomas had been one of them, and now was one of the very few that still walked the physical world.

Lives were lost in fractions of seconds.

This night, the young pale-haired knight came within a single breath of visiting death's gate.

Tomas heard the sword clear its sheath, but in the same moment he heard the first knight move between them, stopping the bloodshed before it began.

Tomas lazily turned back so he faced them.

The woman's eyes burned with the fervor of their order. But she stood as still as a statue, her frozen pose a perfect example of the church's sword techniques. Her master would no doubt be proud.

The first knight's gaze was cold and calculating. He had eyes that missed nothing. Uncertainty flickered across his face as he studied Tomas. After a long moment, he gave a small shake of his head and stood straighter.

Tomas allowed himself to relax a bit.

The girl didn't respond for a moment, then cast furious glances at her partner's back. But she sheathed her sword.

"Be wary," the first knight said. "It's a dangerous town. Just last night a boy was murdered and his killer walks free. If you change your mind, the church is always willing to open its arms and welcome you in its embrace."

Tomas inclined his head, acknowledging the invitation.

The knights then left him alone, returning to their patrol. Tomas watched them walk away.

"A wise man would leave this town and never look back," Elzeth said.

Tomas grunted his agreement. "But aren't you curious?"

"Sure. But I also prefer being alive to dead."

"You're no fun."

Tomas stood there. Another five hundred feet or so and the town would be nothing more than a confusing memory Still...

"There's only one reason I can think of for why the church is so interested in this town," Tomas said.

"I know," Elzeth replied. He sounded grumpy that the thought had occurred to Tomas too.

"And?"

Elzeth paused for a long time. "I'd still rather leave and never look back."

"It'll be fun."

"I haven't had fun since the day we met."

He smiled at Elzeth's customary grouchiness.

Tomas turned so he faced the way he'd come. The section of town he was currently in was too quiet, and he didn't trust the knights. But the gambling halls and saloons weren't much better. Then his eyes alighted on a small place he hadn't paid much attention to earlier, an establishment in the liminal space between order and chaos.

The sign above the door proclaimed that it was an inn.

Perfect.

When he opened the inn's front door, it was as if he'd stepped into a different world, a world of yesteryear that didn't exist anywhere except in the memories of the elders. The entry was quiet, with a space to leave one's footwear. Tomas slipped off his light leather boots and lined them up with the two pairs of sandals already present.

A small basin of water and clean cloths allowed him to wash the dust from his face and hands. He grimaced as the once-clean water turned murky.

The routine, once common but now almost forgotten, served its purpose well. His shoulders relaxed as the cares of the world outside slipped away. He heard the soft footfalls of the innkeeper in the room beyond, but he didn't hurry. The keeper would wait, and Tomas savored the transition from traveler to guest.

When he was ready, Tomas stepped into the next room. There he was greeted by another wonder. The room was austere, so clean Tomas imagined dust trembled at the sight. Each of the four walls held one calligraphic work, each highlighting the four primary virtues of the inn. An older woman knelt at a low table and bowed to him as he entered.

Tomas returned the bow in almost equal measure, then knelt on the other side of the table.

"Good evening, sir," the innkeeper said. "What brings you into town?"

"Good evening. I was just passing through, and hoped you might have food and lodging."

"Just for the night?"

Tomas shrugged. "I might stay a bit. Your town seems like a nice little place."

Her back stiffened, and the expression on her face told him that she was well aware no one called her town a nice place. Her eyes traveled down to the sword at his side. "Might you be looking for employment?" Her tone stole the warmth from the room.

"No ma'am."

Her eyes narrowed, and Tomas suspected that if he'd answered yes she would have shown him the door. As it was, she still might.

Tomas pulled a small but heavy purse from his cloak. He opened it, making sure she saw the gold inside. "How much for two nights, to start?"

He watched her eyes dart from his purse to the door, then back to his purse, where they lingered. Then she smiled and made an entry in the journal before her. The penmanship was the same as the calligraphy on the wall, made up of decisive, confident strokes. "It's a pleasure to welcome you here," she said.

And Tomas almost believed she meant it.

LESS THAN AN HOUR LATER, he was seated in a small dining hall, the only customer. A bottle of wine sat before him, half gone, and Tomas figured dawn couldn't be that far off. He'd never seen a town so active so late into the evening. In his experience, such activity was a conceit of cities, made possible only because of the church's new supplies of power that made the nights as bright as day.

An older gentleman came from the kitchen. Despite his age he moved around the tables with ease, balancing several steaming bowls without problem.

Tomas slid the bottle aside to make room for the food. The sight of it alone nearly brought him to tears. It had been weeks since he'd eaten so well.

"Mind if I join you?" the man asked.

Tomas nodded and poured the innkeeper a glass of wine. They raised their glasses in a silent toast, then drank.

The innkeeper gestured to Tomas' sword, propped against the chair next to Tomas. "My wife believes you're another mercenary."

"Seems to be a common concern in these parts."

"True enough. So are you?"

"Just passing through."

The innkeeper nodded. "You served, didn't you?"

Tomas fixed the older man with a glare, but the innkeeper waved it away. "It's no concern of mine, but I did my time in the war before yours. Just wanted to let you know you have my respect."

"You don't even know what side I was on."

The innkeeper laughed. "Son, if you had been on the winning side, you wouldn't be out here."

Tomas conceded the point.

Elzeth chuckled. "I actually do like him."

So did Tomas. The old man was probably too curious and too observant for his own good, but his intentions were rooted in a good place. The innkeeper extended his hand. "Franz."

Tomas took it. "Tomas."

"I can guess well enough what brought you out here,"

Franz said, "but why stay the night? You don't look like a fool to me."

"Why does the church have four knights here?"

"Eight, actually."

"Eight?"

Franz nodded. "Wondered if that was what had caught your eye. But to answer your question, the short answer is, no one knows."

"And the long version?"

"Takes a bit of telling."

Tomas poured the innkeeper another glass of wine. He ate while Franz talked.

"All started about two years ago," Franz began. "Before that, the town was about as quiet as you'd expect out here. Then Boss Jons arrived."

"Family?" Tomas asked.

"Yes, sir. Brought a small clan with him and took over the town. Drove the marshal off, though he wasn't much anyway. Whole thing was surprisingly peaceful. Only one believer fought it, and he died quick. For the rest of us, we quit paying taxes and started paying protection money. The rates were the same, just a different destination. Life went on, and most of us didn't care one way or another."

"The government never stepped in?"

Franz chuckled. "We're not worth the trouble, and I'm not convinced the marshal ever sounded the alarm. Not sure what they'd do even if they found out, though. All they've got is a handful of marshals, and that won't do nothing."

Tomas nodded.

"Jons drove off most of the people in town, though that wasn't much. Replaced them with his Sons and Daughters. The only ones of us who stayed were the ones too far in debt to leave." Franz gestured around the room. "We love this place, but everything we own is in these walls. Our friends told us to leave as they were packing to go, but we couldn't get anyone to purchase the inn for a fair price. So we stayed."

Franz paused for a breath. "As I said, nothing much changed under Jons. He's tough but fair. We began to get some more Family in town, but Jons kept them well-behaved, and they paid well." Franz hesitated. "But then the first two knights appeared."

"Was there a mission here at the time?"

Franz shook his head.

"Odd."

"Don't even begin to cover it. They show up in the middle of the day, stand in the center of town, and proclaim the whole place is now owned by the church."

The food suddenly tasted bitter in Tomas' mouth. "What?"

Franz shrugged. "Can't rightly explain it myself, but there it was and Jons, well he couldn't have that, for reasons I can't fathom, and he sends the whole Family against them." For several seconds Franz's eyes focused on nothing in particular. "Bloodiest thing I've seen since my service, and maybe even worse. The knights were the best warriors I've ever seen, but Jons had overwhelming numbers. Still, he must have lost more than twenty of his Family that day."

Over twenty Family and two knights? Out here, the land would have to be made of solid gold to justify such numbers. But Tomas believed Franz.

"Since that day, the two sides have been locked in a nearly bloodless duel. Jons put out a call for help. A few Family from the area appeared, but our little town has become a magnet for unsavory types. Whole place is teeming with has-beens all living large off of Jons' gold, and

they don't have the discipline or the respect the Family had."
Franz nodded in the direction of the church-controlled part
of town. "And on the other side, the church is building and
welcoming new believers. They've built a mission and a rest,
and it's all guarded by eight knights and a handful of
soldiers. Feeling most of us have is that there's a battle
coming, far worse than the last. But neither side is confident
they can win yet. So they build up their forces, and we just
wait for the headsman's axe to fall."

Tomas leaned back, the last of his meal finished. It alone
had been worth the cost of the room. Franz was skilled in
the kitchen. "Who do you want to win?"

Franz turned grim at that. "I just want to be left alone
and live in peace." His watchful eyes settled on Tomas. "But
I think you understand that well enough, don't you?"

Tomas nodded.

Franz stood up and began clearing the dishes off the
table. But he hesitated before carrying them away. He
looked like a man torn between two desires. Finally, he
gestured toward Tomas' sword. "You any good with that?"

"Yes."

"Figured. I wouldn't normally ask, but there's been some
trouble the past few days over my granddaughter, who lives
here with us. She's almost of age, and usually serves the
meals, but the hour is late and my wife didn't trust you after
everything that's been going on. The girl could use your
protection. We can't pay much, but we would do what we
could to make it worth your time."

Tomas was tempted. He liked Franz. But he'd seen
enough trouble for several lifetimes, and he'd learned not to
invite more in. "Sorry, but I'm just passing through."

Franz sagged as though he'd been punched. But there

was steel in his spine yet. He quickly straightened. "I understand. But please, consider it while you're with us."

Tomas grimaced, and Franz pressed harder.

"She's a principled girl. We've raised her as we did our own daughter. But I fear that if she has no protection, she will have no choice but to take her own life before the week is done."

4

Tomas woke to the sun streaming through the slit between his curtains. He blinked and rolled into a sitting position, then rubbed his eyes and yawned. Though he'd had one of the latest nights he could remember, the night and morning of rest had more than made up for it.

He noticed the quiet. Though it had to be almost noon, there were none of the usual noises of a town at work. He stood and pushed the curtains aside, revealing what might as well have been a ghost town.

Tomas watched the street for a while, but there was precious little to see. Eventually he closed the curtains and began working through the forms of the sword school he had been raised in. He'd long ago lost count of the number of repetitions of each form he'd performed in his life, but he assumed the answer was well into the tens of thousands. The temptation after so many years was to simply perform the movements without thought. Every cut, parry, and turn was already inscribed deep in his body. He could probably perform most of the forms blackout drunk and blindfolded.

But that was sloppy mental and physical discipline.

His masters had taught him better than that.

And that was why he was both still alive and free, while most he had served with were not.

He brought his full attention to his forms. He noted any tightness in his body and judged each cut as though supervised by his strictest master. In time his mind fell into rhythm with his body. Even without Elzeth, his senses sharpened.

The boundary that separated him from the world slowly dissolved. With every cut, the man named Tomas faded. No longer was he alone in a small inn within an unnamed town. He became part of something larger, something almost indefinable. The fire in his stomach grew hotter, fueled by the winds of his practice.

He stopped when he heard the soft footsteps on the first stair of the stairwell leading to his room.

He tried to hold onto the feeling his practice had created for a few more precious moments. He didn't allow many to witness his practice, but those who did always assumed his dedication and focus were due to a desire to keep his skills as sharp as his sword.

The assumption wasn't wrong.

It was just incomplete.

His practice brought him a sense of peace. Of wholeness.

Gifts far more valuable than prowess on a battlefield.

He sheathed his sword and rested it against a wall. Given the pace and lightness of the footsteps, he had a good guess who approached.

The loud, firm knock on the door was a stark contrast to the light steps. It surprised him. "Come in."

The young woman entered like a storm, blowing away

the last vestiges of Tomas' serenity. She stood tall, with long dark hair and eyes that sparked, as though she was looking for a fight. She carried a serving tray filled with bread, butter, tea, and water, but she made no effort to balance it. His breakfast wildly tilted from side to side, and he gave himself even odds of either enjoying the meal or picking it up off the floor.

Somehow the tray made it to the small table in the corner of the room without spilling even a drop of its contents. Task complete, the woman fixed him with a stare. "We heard you moving around, so Grandda sent me up with the food."

Tomas bowed. "Thank you."

She frowned.

He expected her to turn and leave. She clearly wasn't interested in serving him up to the standards the inn claimed to uphold.

But she stood there, in his room, openly studying him. Though nearly unspeakably rude, considering the context, she didn't hide her action. Then she scowled and said, "That's it?"

Tomas looked around the room, but it held no answers for him. He didn't need to pretend to be puzzled.

"Grandda told me he asked for your help. Said you turned him down. Which is why he sent me up instead of Grandma. The old schemer wants me to change your mind. Hells, he'd probably be happy if you proposed. He has a soft spot for young men who served."

Tomas smiled at the thought of the traditional grandparents raising this brash young woman. "Your grandda told me last night you weren't of age."

She looked down at herself, then back at him.

He shrugged and her scowl deepened. "I'm sorry for

your troubles, but I truly don't seek conflict." He paused. "But why lie to me?"

Whatever anger she had built up on the journey to his room vanished. She sank into Tomas' chair, oblivious to the fact she was preventing him from eating the meal she'd brought up for him. He looked longingly at the fresh bread.

"Grandda is a man torn by competing desires," she said. "He knows how badly I wish to travel east, and so he sometimes searches for appropriate suitors. His attempts have gotten more desperate as things have gotten worse here. But he also wants me close. I'm the only family left to them."

"You're of age," Tomas said, "so why not find your own escort?"

She scoffed. "Look around. Most everyone coming through is either with the church or the Family. If they aren't, they're looking to get hired by one side or the other." Her eyes fell. "And the last young man who stood up for me got a knife in the back as his reward."

Tomas thought of the grieving parents. "And your grandparents won't move?"

She shook her head. "This place means everything to them. They've invested everything into it. And the only potential buyers would be the church or the Family, and Grandda refuses to sell to either. Neither would pay much, anyway."

Tomas shrugged. Better to be broke and free than wealthy and in chains. But few people he met felt the same.

She sat in silence for a minute, then shifted her weight and batted her eyes at him. "So, will you be the one to take me away from here, stranger?"

Her exaggerated manner implied it wasn't a serious offer, but her eyes told a different story.

If he said yes, she would join him.

She'd do almost anything to leave this town.

He shook his head. She was an attractive young woman, and he admired her spirit, but it wouldn't work. "I'm heading west."

She scrunched up her face. "There's nothing out there."

"Exactly."

She studied him one last time, then stood up, her decision made. "My name is Inaya."

"Tomas."

"I'll leave you to your meal, then, Tomas."

He bowed in thanks, but before she could leave, a loud pounding echoed from the main door.

Inaya's face turned whiter than the uniforms of the knights. She ran to the window and looked down on the street. She swore, and Tomas heard the main door being pulled open. A commotion ensued downstairs.

She turned to him, glancing quickly at his sword. "Wait here. If you want to live, please don't interfere."

With that, she was out the door and gone.

5

M

ore commotion erupted downstairs. Tomas heard the crash of something heavy, followed by Inaya shouting, her voice was sharp enough to cut stone.

Tomas walked over to where his sword rested and picked it up. Within seconds it was at his hip where it belonged. He went to the window and gently pulled aside the curtain.

Two enormous men stood just outside the inn. Their arms were crossed and they had their backs to the building, preventing anyone from interfering.

Not that anyone would. Not if everyone was either Family or church.

Tomas listened to the sounds of struggle as they continued below.

The men outside were Family. Their tattoos marked them easily enough. Both shifted their weight from side to side, and one kept looking back at the inn whenever the ruckus became too loud.

Tomas didn't think they wanted to be a part of this.

"Are we getting involved?" Elzeth asked.

"Rather not," Tomas replied.

Elzeth snorted, then went silent.

He waited, watched, and listened. Perhaps this would all end up amounting to nothing.

And perhaps he would catch a shooting star before supper.

Eiro came out of the inn, pulling Inaya behind him by her hair. Franz followed, blood trickling from the corner of his mouth. He said something, his hand reaching out to Inaya. Eiro turned suddenly and planted a vicious kick in the innkeeper's chest. Franz almost flew backward.

Tomas' grip on his sword tightened.

Franz was back on his feet faster than Tomas would have expected from a man his age.

"You with me?" Tomas asked.

"For this? Sure," Elzeth said.

Tomas took the stairs three at a time, feet landing softly on each one.

The entrance was a disaster. The basin had been knocked over, spilling water everywhere. Long gashes had been cut by a sword across two walls. Franz's wife's head was only inches underneath one such cut. She was propped up against the wall, her eyes unfocused. Drying blood covered her face. Most looked like it had come from her nose.

But she was breathing steadily, so Tomas walked right by her.

He walked through the open door just in time to watch Eiro kick Franz once again.

The old innkeeper was curled into a ball, as if trying to protect something valuable. Eiro kicked and kicked, but for all the violence, Tomas didn't think the young man was doing much damage. Franz was tough as gristle, even if age had stolen the speed he needed to defeat his assailant.

Tomas didn't even break his stride. His right arm came back as his hips and torso twisted. Eiro's focus on beating Franz cost him his awareness. Tomas unleashed his strike, his whole body uncoiling behind his open palm.

Eiro noticed the movement just in time to watch the bottom of Tomas' palm meet his chest. His eyes opened wide as his feet left the ground. His hand came out of Inaya's hair.

The blow sent Eiro crashing into the dirt directly between the two large men he'd brought with him. They turned like lumbering behemoths, and Tomas wondered if they were quick enough to hit anything that moved faster than a cow.

Elzeth laughed at the thought.

Tomas turned to Franz and helped him up. He felt the old man's wiry muscle, still firm after all these years. A few superficial cuts and a split lip lent Franz a fearsome visage, but Tomas saw no wounds that concerned him.

Eiro struggled to his feet. He appeared to be struggling for breath, and he leaned against one of his brothers for support. "You shouldn't have done that, stranger," he wheezed.

Tomas looked Franz over one more time, but the innkeeper waved away the attention. "I'll be fine," he said.

Then Tomas turned to Inaya. He could feel Eiro's seething hatred, radiating off him like heat from a kettle left too long over the flame. But the boy could stew for a while longer. "Did he hurt you?"

Inaya's face was pale, her attention mostly focused on the Family. But she shook her head in answer to his question.

If Eiro lived today, it would be because of that answer.

"Hey! I'm talking to you!" Eiro shouted, as if he wasn't sure his voice could travel the six feet between them.

Tomas turned slowly until he faced the three Family.

Eiro's two brothers looked uncertain. No doubt, this hadn't been how they expected their afternoon to go. But they were below Eiro in the hierarchy, as they made no move without his order.

"You have a death wish, stranger?" Eiro asked.

Tomas didn't reply.

Eiro misunderstood his silence. "Too scared to talk?" A malicious grin spread across his face. "Then I'll give you one last chance to live. Get on your hands and knees. Clean the dust off my boots with your tongue. You do good enough, I might let you live." Eiro put his hand on the sword that was too big for him. The sword he'd stolen from the young man he'd killed.

Tomas remained silent.

Eiro's two brothers looked more uncertain than ever. They might move as slow as oxen, but they recognized Tomas as a predator.

Most prey did.

Eiro snarled. "Kill him, brothers."

They hesitated, but they had pledged their lives to the Family. In so doing, they had forfeited their freedom to choose. Tomas understood those like Eiro's brothers. They believed that the certainty such loyalty conferred was well worth the loss of choice and responsibility.

Though he hadn't recognized it at the time, it had been the same reason he'd first volunteered to serve. The certainty of three meals a day and steady pay made following the orders and routines of the military well worth it.

For a while.

So Tomas took pity on Eiro's brothers as they drew their swords. He chose to believe they would have left him alone, had it been up to them.

They advanced, one lumbering step at a time.

"No!" Inaya screamed.

But events were already in motion. They had their own momentum, tumbling toward their conclusion like a boulder rolling down the side of a mountain.

Tomas struck first. He darted forward, an eye on the drawn swords. There was some slight chance the brothers had hoped to mislead him by their earlier slowness, so he remained wary.

He needn't have bothered.

Eiro's brothers were as slow and untrained as they had appeared. Perhaps most problems in their small town could be solved by their meaty fists, but against Tomas they might as well have been standing still.

Tomas struck, a combination of fists, elbows, and knees, all aimed at soft spots.

He didn't miss.

Eiro's brothers collapsed.

They would be fine. Tomas hadn't even knocked them unconscious. But it would take them a few minutes to move again. Perhaps they would make better choices in the future.

Elzeth yawned.

Tomas turned his attention to Eiro.

The poor boy was stuck between two difficult futures. He could run, but the retreat would be witnessed by his brothers. He would lose considerable face in the Family. Or he could attack. But some part of his foolish mind was starting to realize that maybe he had picked a fight with an opponent he couldn't beat.

Life or honor?

Tomas knew which mattered more.

But Eiro disagreed.

Tomas watched the boy's emotions play across his face, as easy to read as Franz's wife's calligraphy. Eiro experienced a few moments of fear as he understood what Tomas had done to his brothers.

The easiest person to fool was yourself.

Tomas could well imagine the stories that flooded Eiro's disbelieving mind: Eiro was stronger than his brothers. Eiro was stronger than anyone. What he had seen was nothing more than a mistake. There was no way the stranger was this skilled.

So Eiro drew his stolen sword and sealed his fate.

The boy had some training, but far more confidence than his skill warranted. Even without the oversized sword that he swung too slow, Eiro wouldn't have had a chance.

Tomas stepped to meet Eiro's charge. He drew and cut in a single motion, and they passed one another.

Inaya gasped.

He turned in time to see Eiro fall, a dark pool of blood mixing into the dirt of the road. Tomas almost spit in disgust. Eiro had deserved his fate, but it was still a waste.

He walked over to the boy. Eiro only had a minute or so to live. He snapped the blood off his blade and sheathed the weapon. Then he squatted down next to the boy. Tomas spoke softly, ignoring Eiro's whimpering and the desperate fear in his eyes.

From the One we became many;
  To the One we return.
  May the gates beyond
  Welcome your weary soul.

· · ·

TOMAS WAITED for the boy to die. He witnessed Eiro's final breath, then gently closed Eiro's unseeing eyes. He took the sword from Eiro's hand and inspected it for blood. When he was sure it was clean, he untied the sheath from Eiro's side and sheathed the stolen weapon.

He put the sword down reverently in front of one of Eiro's brothers. The man's eyes went wide.

"Return this to the parents of the man it belonged to, please."

The man nodded.

Tomas stood up and walked back toward the inn. Inaya appeared to be frozen in shock, her eyes locked on the scene in the street. But she would be fine. He spoke to Franz. "Am I still welcome in your inn?"

Franz only hesitated for a moment. "You paid for two nights, so yes." He grimaced. "But you might want to consider running. As fast and as far as your feet can carry you. A horse would be best."

Tomas frowned. "You're paying the Family protection money. Eiro's behavior violated their own code."

Franz shook his head. "It's not why you killed him that's the trouble. It's who he was."

Tomas looked back at the body. "Who was he?"

"Boss Jons' eldest son," Franz replied.

6

Tomas went back inside the inn. Franz's wife was already on her feet and cleaning up the mess Eiro had made. When Tomas entered, she bowed deeply to him. He returned the gesture and used the water from the now-upright basin to wash his feet. The dust from his bare feet turned the bottom of the basin to mud. Tomas grimaced and turned to Franz's wife. He was about to offer to clean the basin, but from the look on her face, such an offer would be an insult to her hospitality.

He bowed again. "Tell me when Jons arrives. I'll meet him outside."

She nodded in gratitude.

Tomas climbed the stairs to his room. He sat at the table and broke into the bread that Inaya left for him.

It wasn't warm anymore, but it was still excellent. He'd noticed, back when he'd begun his journey, that most inns out east didn't serve simple bread anymore. With so many inns to choose from, innkeepers sought ways to distinguish themselves from the competition. As a result, Tomas had endured breads stuffed to bursting with various fruit and nuts, each loaf more complicated than the last.

This bread was a welcome departure. A few ingredients, prepared with experience and care. It was what bread should be. He respected Franz's wife, even if the feeling wasn't mutual.

He'd barely finished his breakfast when there was a soft knock on his door. "Jons is coming," Inaya said from the other side.

Tomas stood and opened the door. "Thank you. And thank you for the breakfast. It was delicious."

He ignored her disbelieving stare as he stepped into the hallway and down the stairs. He didn't want to confront Jons inside the inn, which meant he didn't have time to speak with Inaya.

Both Franz and his wife were waiting for him in the entryway. Tomas nodded when he saw them. "Thank you for breakfast. Your bread is some of the best I've ever tasted."

Though her hands trembled, Franz's wife smiled with pride.

Franz wasn't so easily distracted. He spoke as Tomas pulled on his boots. "There's still time to run. He's bringing his six best swords with him, and rumor has it that none are as good as him. We can delay them."

Tomas gave the couple a short bow, then stepped outside, ignoring Franz's inarticulate cry of protest. He walked to the middle of the street. Eiro's body was gone, most likely carried away by his two brothers. But his blood had caked into the dirt of the street.

A group approached from the east, where the gambling halls now stood quiet.

Even from their gait, Tomas could see this group was far more dangerous than the last. He glanced up and looked at the watchtowers. Both the church's and the Family's watchers were focused on him.

They weren't alone. He saw curtains parting and shadows moving in windows along the street. He'd rarely had such an audience, even if the street itself was nearly deserted.

Boss Jons and his guards stopped a dozen paces away. Jons was lanky, with untamed dark hair. Tattoos ran up his arms, and if not for his eyes, Tomas might have dismissed him. He didn't look like a man who could control a clan of Family and the town.

But looking into his eyes, Tomas sensed hidden depths to the man. There was an implacability within, a calm that only existed because of the storms he had weathered. Not to mention a sharp intelligence.

Elzeth was active, sharpening Tomas' senses. Against all seven, Tomas would need the aid.

But the guards were relaxed.

Ready to fight, but not expecting one.

Tomas relaxed in response.

A stiff breeze kicked up a bit of dust between him and the Family.

Jons stepped forward, outside his ring of guards. He offered a short bow to Tomas. If any of the guards were surprised that Jons would bow to the man who killed his son, they didn't show it.

Tomas returned the gesture in equal measure.

Jons looked up and down the street. "Is there a place we may speak more privately?"

"The drink at the inn is excellent."

Jons inclined his head, and Tomas led the way inside. He turned his back on Jons, but listened for any sudden movements.

They entered without incident.

Franz's whole family was there. They scurried back when Jons entered. Tomas spoke to Franz. "We would like a place to talk alone. With your best wine."

Franz looked uncertain, but bowed and hurried off.

Tomas went through the ritual of cleaning his hands and face, noting the basin had been once again filled with clean water. Jons did the same, and they both took off their shoes as they entered.

Jons stared at the walls where his son had done his damage. He bowed to Franz's wife. "I'm sorry, Elissa. Later, I will speak with you and Franz about recompense."

Elissa bowed. "You are too kind, sir."

The response was rote, and Tomas thought he caught a flicker of something pass across Jons' face. Distaste? He couldn't be sure. It had happened too quickly. Without his sharpened senses, he wasn't sure he would have noticed at all.

Franz reappeared and led them to the dining room. There, in a corner, was a table set up with two chairs, several cups, and a bottle of wine.

"Thank you, Franz," Jons said. "Now please leave us."

Franz bowed deeply and left.

They took their seats across from one another. Tomas poured the wine and lifted his cup in a silent toast. Jons joined him, and they each took a sip.

It was good. Not quite as good as the wine he'd been carrying earlier, but rich and flavorful all the same.

He waited for Jons.

And waited some more.

The silence didn't seem to bother the boss, but it didn't bother Tomas either. And the wine was good.

Finally, Jons spoke. "They tell me you said the old words for my son as he died."

Tomas nodded.

"Thank you."

"He deserved no less."

The barest hint of a smile played upon Jons' lips. "Few would have felt the same. And even less would have done as you did."

It was probably true, but also rude to agree. Tomas took another sip of his wine, and Jons mirrored him.

"He was my blood," Jons said, "but he was my wife's child. I mourn his passing, but he was obstinate, entitled, and cruel. I ordered him to drop his pursuit of Inaya after he killed the boy, but he disobeyed me. His actions dishonor both me and the Family. But what else could I have done? He was my son, and my firstborn, too old to be disciplined like a child."

Tomas had no answers, but he didn't think Jons was looking for any. Jons spoke matter-of-factly.

They drank again, and Tomas refilled their cups.

"The Family needs this town. We've got some of our best here, and we're hiring everyone who is willing and has a sword. But the church has their knights. I've tried to protect and run this town well, to keep the people on our side. But those like Eiro made my task next to impossible."

Jons watched him for reactions, but Tomas revealed nothing.

The boss tried a different approach. "You served, didn't you? Near the end."

Tomas knew it was a guess based off his age, skill, and direction of travel, but it was a good one. And there was little to be gained by lying. "I did."

"So did I. Near the beginning."

That piece of information caught Tomas by surprise. "Really?"

"I wasn't Family then."

So he had married in, then. To the wife who had allowed Eiro's behavior. And within a few years of marrying into the Family, he'd been sent to this town and given incredible resources. Tomas eyed the warrior across from him in a new light.

Jons was an interesting man. Cold as ice, but as ambitious a man as Tomas had ever met.

"What was the name of your unit?" Jons asked.

"Didn't have one."

"Ah," Jons said. "One of those."

Tomas nodded.

"Then that makes this much easier." Jons leaned forward. "My wife will want blood. Eiro was her reason for living. I don't want to guess the number of Family it would take to kill you, but the number is too high. If we move against you, we'll be too weak to take on the church. So there's only one way out of this mess. And only one way for you to have a chance at surviving your visit to this town."

Tomas suppressed a shiver. He'd killed this man's son. Eiro's blood still stained the street. And Jons viewed him as nothing more than a piece in a larger game, or part of an equation that needed to be balanced. "What's that?"

"You need to join us in our fight against the church."

7

Tomas followed Jons to the front of the inn, where they once again came across Elissa. Tomas took out his purse and pressed some coins into her hand. "Please keep my room for a few more nights."

Jons raised an eyebrow but said nothing.

The six Family remained in the street. They didn't look like they had moved since Jons stepped into the inn. The boss stopped Tomas before they reached the guards. He spoke low. "My wife will not approve of my decision, and there are some in the Family who still consider me an outsider."

"I understand," Tomas said. Boss Jons fought battles both at home and in the streets.

Jons then took his place in the center of the six guards, but Tomas didn't join him. He refused to voluntarily place himself in the middle of so many well-trained warriors.

"And yet you're walking into a hall where you'll be surrounded by so many more," Elzeth pointed out.

"If you have a better idea, I'm listening. And anyway, you're just as curious."

Elzeth had no retort to that.

Tomas followed the Family to the row of gambling halls. Jons made straight for the largest of them, a two-story building expansive enough to fit several of Franz's inns. Inside, a handful of staff bustled around, cleaning and preparing the place for another wild night. Tomas saw tables for both dice and cards. His hand twitched at the memories of nights he'd spent in such places long years ago. He'd won and lost several fortunes over his years of service.

Then he noticed the activity was limited to the front of the house. In the back, a group stood in a silent circle. Tomas could guess what drew their attention.

A woman of average build, wearing a black dress, turned at their entrance. Her eyes were rimmed with red, and tears had left streaks down her cheeks. When she saw Jons and Tomas, she sneered.

She stormed toward them. All activity in the hall ground to a quiet halt. Every eye turned to the drama unfolding near the center of the house.

Her voice was cold, filled with barely restrained fury. "Why is *he* here?"

"I've hired him." Jons met his wife's rage with a calm strength.

For a second, Tomas worried the air between them might catch fire. He'd fought in wars and broken hearts, but he'd never seen a stare filled with so much venom. The silence in the hall carried a weight. Even the air was perfectly still. No one dared breathe and unbalance the situation.

The woman's hand snapped up and slapped Jons across the face.

Jons saw it coming. Tomas tracked the movement of the boss's eyes. But he let it hit. For all the strength she'd put into the blow, it barely affected the boss. She spat at his feet. "Coward." Then she fixed Tomas with an equally terrifying glare.

She turned on her heels and returned to the body of her firstborn. Jons made no move to stop her.

He spoke before she returned to the group. His voice carried, loud and clear, through the hall. "Family! Tonight we strike." Jons held the gaze of anyone who dared meet his eye. "Let everyone know. We gather here when Tolkin rises. It is time to end this."

The hall cleared out except for the mourners in the back. Jons looked at Tomas. "I'll show you to a room."

Tomas followed Jons up a flight of stairs. The upper floor of the hall was filled with rooms, most of them little more than bunk beds and a small chest for storage. Jons passed those and slid open the door to a nicer room. A wide bed and ornate table distinguished it.

"It's probably best if you remain here until tonight," Jons said. The boss appeared to have his mind firmly focused on other matters. "Can you best a knight?"

Tomas debated whether or not to speak true. No small part of his survival hinged on people underestimating him. But he suspected Jons had a decent idea of his skill already. Otherwise, there would have been far more violence when they first met. "Yes."

"More than one?"

"Probably, but I'd rather not have to."

A hint of a smile played across Jons' face. "Is there anything you need? Food, drink, company?"

Food tempted him, but Tomas shook his head.

"Very well. I'll come for you tonight."

Tomas nodded and Jons left.

"Thoughts?" Tomas asked.

"He's sharp. But he's not a leader. Not the sort of man people want to follow. He's got no heart," Elzeth said.

"I still get the sense he's the only person keeping this town from falling into chaos."

"It would be peaceful enough if the church took over."

Tomas snorted and circled the room. His lodgings seemed safe enough, at least for the moment. He trusted Jons, to an extent. The rest of the Family would obey the boss for now, whether they liked it or not. Coups weren't unheard of inside the Family, but they were unusual. But if Jons finished the fight against the church tonight, his position would be secure. No one would overthrow the man who won the town.

Tomas sat on the edge of the bed.

"If you're going to leave, it needs to be now. Jons can't pursue you, not without losing everything else," Elzeth said.

Tomas rubbed his forehead. "What do you think?"

Elzeth was silent for several minutes. But there was no hesitation in his voice when he answered. "We stay."

Tomas nodded. "Stop them all?"

"We can't let the Family have it either."

Tomas swore. "So much for a quiet trip."

"You were getting bored, anyway."

"I was enjoying being bored."

Tomas slid from the bed to the floor and sat cross-legged. He closed his eyes. "Let's find out where we stand. Can you find her?"

He winced as his hearing sharpened. Footsteps from the main hall sounded like war drums. Distant voices thundered in his head. Despite the pain, he listened. Some of the Family were busy enjoying company. Others sipped at drinks, steeling their nerves for the battle to come. Still others spoke in low tones with one another, speculating on the fight.

Then he was in a room. Several people were breathing, but the room was otherwise quiet. A door slid open, then closed again. Footsteps hurried across the wood floor and Tomas heard someone take a kneeling or sitting position. Then all was quiet again.

The voice that spoke was familiar. "My son's death must be avenged."

Another voice answered. "They say he is strong."

"I have no doubt. He must have been, to defeat Eiro. And my husband sees his first duty as defeating the church. His decision is unprincipled, but I understand it. However, there are many paths to revenge."

"Ma'am?"

"No one from the Family should dishonor themselves with this task. It goes against my husband's implied wishes. But spilled blood has its own claim on honor. We need mercenaries. Are there any we've hired that are skilled?"

A third voice spoke. Tomas memorized the sound of each voice, so he would know those who were in Jons' wife's inner circle. "There are half a dozen or so. One is perhaps even strong enough to best some of the boss's guards."

"Find them. Tonight, well before Tolkin rises, they should go to Franz's inn. Tell them they may indulge in whatever brutality they wish. But when they appear at my husband's meeting, I expect to know that the whole family is dead. They've been a thorn in our side for long enough. Tell the mercenaries there will be plenty of coin in it, and they can keep whatever they loot."

Weight shifted, and Tomas guessed it was someone bowing. Then he heard footsteps and the sound of the door opening and closing, as the messenger departed bearing their cruel orders.

"To the rest of you, spread the message among those who are loyal. The swordsman must fight tonight. I fear my husband is right in that. But when his usefulness has ended, I want his head."

She paused.

"Make sure everyone knows that if he survives the battle tonight, I will be most displeased."

8

The sounds faded until they returned to normal. In Tomas' room, near the back of the building, all was quiet. He opened his eyes and took a deep breath. "I'm beginning to think she doesn't like me," he said.

"She has illustrious company," Elzeth replied.

Tomas didn't move from his spot on the floor. He made plans, then picked them apart as best he could. Elzeth helped, the dance familiar to them both. Nothing they imagined was perfect, but nothing ever was.

Tomas stood and stretched, then bounced lightly on his feet. "Ready?"

"Sure," Elzeth said.

Tomas went to the window in his room and peered out. As he'd expected, neither watchtower was in sight. He opened the window, looked around one last time, then dropped. He landed without a sound.

His first challenge was getting back to Franz's inn without being spotted by the Family watchtower. Had Tomas enjoyed the gift of foresight, he would have mentally mapped out the town earlier, but he'd never expected events to gather momentum so quickly.

He kept to the shadows and moved steadily west. Narrow alleys kept him safe from the watchtower's gaze. When he did have to cross a street he first ensured it was clear, then hurried across.

If this town had been anything like the dozens of others he'd passed through, his attempts at stealth would have been laughable. But most of the town remained asleep, still worn out from the night before. Returning to the gambling hall would be another problem, but hopefully by then he would enjoy the cover of darkness.

He reached the back wall of Franz's inn. A palisade had been dug deep into the ground, rising perhaps a dozen feet in the air. The tops of each post had been sharpened to points. He grunted. An impressive barrier for a small inn.

Tomas looked around. There was nothing for it. If he tried the main door he was certain he would be noticed.

So he jumped, clearing the sharpened stakes easily and landing silently on the other side.

It was as if he had jumped into another world. He'd landed near a rock garden. A few small, no doubt hardy, shrubs had been placed throughout the garden, and patterns raked around them. The whole space inspired a sense of tranquility. Tomas dropped into a squat and admired the garden for several minutes. The care that had been used in its creation was evident. Even the shrubs were precisely trimmed.

The garden didn't feel like Elissa's work. Her calligraphy was firm and unyielding. The defining aspect of the garden was its adaptability. How it used the space available to the greatest effect. This was Franz.

But both partners were masters of their chosen crafts.

Tomas stood, sad that such a treasure was hidden from the world. There were few left who appreciated such efforts, and most of those were of a generation passing away.

He leaped clear across the garden in a single bound, unwilling to damage Franz's work in any way. Then he knocked on the back door. When no one answered, he knocked again.

This time he heard footsteps on the other side. It opened, and Inaya greeted him. She frowned at the sight. "What are you doing here?"

"I came to speak with your family."

She debated for a moment with herself, then stood aside and let him in. She played with her hair as he passed. "Tomas—"

He turned.

"Thank you." She gave him a short bow, then gestured to the dining room.

"You're welcome." The warm atmosphere of the inn set his mind at ease. His decision had been made. He found Franz and Elissa in the dining hall. They both stared, eyes blank, into the distance, lost in thought.

They startled when they noticed him. Elissa fixed him with a hard stare, but Franz stood to pour him a drink. "You working for the Family now?"

Tomas chose not to respond. He took a sip from the offered glass. The drink burned his throat. "I need you to find whoever is in charge of the knights and bring them here. Fast."

Elissa slapped her hand on the bar and stood. She stormed out of the room and then out the front door.

"When I married her," Franz said, "the first promise she made me give her was that I would leave the service as soon as I could. She detests violence. She's grateful, though."

"How are you?"

"I've been hit harder by angry children."

Tomas chuckled.

"How did you get over our wall?"

Their eyes met. Franz suspected the truth. Tomas made no reply. Then the old innkeeper nodded. "I see."

"Does it change anything?"

Franz shook his head. "Not in this inn. How long have you—?"

"A long time. Before the war."

"I didn't think anyone survived that long."

Tomas shrugged. "Most don't."

Franz looked to the door his wife had left through. "No one knows what's about to happen here, do they?"

"You should leave," Tomas said.

"We'll discuss it," Franz said, "but this is our home. We built it with our own hands."

The main door opened, and soon Elissa escorted in the two knights Tomas had run into the night before. They stiffened when they saw him. Tomas held up his hands in a gesture of peace. "I have information for you."

The tall knight, apparently the commander, stepped forward. "What kind of information?"

"Boss Jons is gathering his forces to attack you tonight," Tomas said.

"Why?"

"Because he offered to pay me very well to join them. And with me, he believes he can win."

The younger woman went for her sword, but her commander's outstretched arm stopped her. "So why tell us?"

"Because I believe in fighting fair. And it's only fair to give you a chance to hire my services as well."

The second knight turned a shade of red Tomas hadn't known was possible for a human. Her whole body trembled. A true believer, too young for even the smallest doubts to have crept into her soul. She wanted to kill him something fierce.

The commander eyed Tomas coolly. "And you would join us, just for money?"

"There's also the slight problem that Jons' wife wants to see me dead for murdering her son. Figured it might be worth being on the side of the church if she's after me."

The commander shook his head. "You aren't a believer. The church will not ally itself with the likes of you."

His partner's face nearly shone with pride.

Tomas raised his glass. "Fair enough. Figured I'd give you the chance, though. But that attack is still coming tonight. Not long after Tolkin rises. Be ready."

The commander nodded, then turned and left. Tomas watched them go as he sipped at his drink.

Once they were gone, Franz spoke. "Just what are you playing at?"

Tomas stood, stretched, and yawned. "You keep the room open for me?"

Franz nodded.

"Good. Your town is too exciting. I think I'm going to lie down and take a nap. Try to make sure I'm not disturbed. And if you can find something white for me to wear later tonight, I'd greatly appreciate it."

He climbed the stairs to his room and lay down. The sun was just beginning to fall.

When it completed its journey for the day, the real fighting would begin.

9

Elzeth woke him as the sun neared the horizon. He stood, stretched, and ran through a quick handful of his forms. He stopped when he heard footsteps on the stairs.

Elissa's knock was softer than he expected. When he opened the door he found her standing in the hall, white cloth bundled in her arms. She thrust it at him.

Tomas accepted and unfurled it. The stitching was well done, and even if it wouldn't fool anyone standing close, he wasn't worried. He only needed to mislead the watchers in the Family tower. "Thank you."

Elissa scowled. "Not sure what it is you're planning, but I want no more part of it. My husband, for reasons I can't fathom, believes you're going to change things around here. Now, don't get me wrong. I'm grateful for you coming to my granddaughter's aid, but when I look at you I only see another murderer. Sure, you've got more control than any of the other killers flooding this town, but I told Franz that just makes you the worst of the bunch. And you know what he did?"

Tomas took half a step back under the verbal assault. He raised his hands in surrender and shook his head.

"He just sat there and smiled as if he's in on some sort of secret. I don't like it, and I don't like you, not one bit!"

Tomas kept the smile from his face.

Fortunately, Elissa's anger was like a spring thunderstorm. It developed quickly but blew out almost as fast. She'd said what she wanted to say, so she turned to leave.

"You're not wrong," Tomas said, halting her in her tracks, "and Franz is fortunate to have you as his wife."

Elissa shifted her weight from side to side, torn between staying and leaving. Her indecision didn't last long. She planted herself outside his door. "Don't think your flattering ways are going to change my mind."

Tomas grinned. "I wouldn't dream of it."

"So, what are you up to?"

"Jons' wife is sending mercenaries here tonight to take revenge for Eiro's death. I plan to stop them."

Elissa bit her lower lip. "That woman has a cruel streak a mile long, but she's no fool, and she's thorough. She'll send a large party."

"I told Franz to run."

She chuckled at that. "My husband has never run in his life. I'm surprised he isn't sharpening his old sword as we speak."

"I don't think he'll be needed."

Elissa eyed him. "Well, I'll say one thing for you. You certainly don't lack in confidence. But can you back up all those big words?"

"I intend to."

She sighed. "Franz is a better judge of such things than I am. All you lost warriors out west just look like sad puppies to me. But Franz can spot the wolves." She looked him up and down again. "Seems to me you could use a bit more meat on your bones, though."

"If your husband keeps cooking for me, that won't be hard."

That finally elicited a deep laugh. It was the first he'd heard from her. "You speak true there, son. Franz tells me he was quite the soldier back in the day, but it was his skill in the kitchen that won me over. If I have one piece of advice for young men these days, it's to put down the swords and pick up the kitchen knives. Whole world would be a better place for it."

"Someday, I'd like to do that," Tomas said.

Her mirth vanished as she looked down at the cloth he held. "You're going to start a whole mess of trouble with that."

"I hope so."

"Why?"

"I don't like seeing people being made to kneel. Especially not out here."

Elissa nodded. "I see why my husband likes you." She turned to go down the stairs. "Don't go getting yourself killed now. I'm just starting to think you aren't half bad."

He watched her go, then looked out the window of his room. The sun was just touching the horizon, and Tomas figured his time was running short. He threw on the white clothing, making sure it covered all his other clothes. Then he went downstairs. Franz stood in the entryway, watching the street. Tomas sat down a few feet away and waited.

The mercenaries didn't keep them long. "They're coming," Franz said. "There's got to be nearly a dozen of them."

Tomas frowned. Elissa had been right. Jons' wife took no chances. That was more than he'd expected.

Quite a few more.

Elzeth grew more active. "We're going to have a proper fight on our hands," he said.

"Are you sure you don't want help?" Franz asked. "I might not be young anymore, but I've still got a fight or two left in me."

Tomas actually considered it. A dozen was a lot.

Then he shook his head.

Franz looked doubtful about the decision, but he didn't object.

Tomas stepped out of the inn and waited for the mercenaries in the street. It was nearly the same place he'd fought Eiro earlier in the day. The nearest of the mercenaries, a short man with a scar on his right cheek, stopped ten feet away. He frowned, as if he didn't quite understand what he was seeing. "Who are you?"

Tomas drew his sword, and Elzeth caught fire within him. He gritted his teeth against the familiar onslaught of energy. Even after all their years together, he was never fully prepared for Elzeth's abilities.

He walked forward, the pace painfully slow. But they were being watched. If he covered the distance too quickly, suspicions would grow.

The scarred man pointed his blade and yelled, and mercenaries closed in from both sides. Many grinned viciously at the idea of an easy kill. Only the scarred man remained behind, his eyes wary.

They were all too slow, but those on Tomas' right were the slowest. He angled toward them, choosing to thin the herd quickly. Several swords rose, their owners expecting to strike him down with a simple overhead cut. Now that he was among them, he moved faster, ignoring their wild attacks. In the confusion of battle, the watchtowers wouldn't notice his speed as easily.

One warrior was wiser than the others. The point of his sword stabbed for Tomas' heart, but Tomas spun around the tip faster than the mercenary could react. He used the momentum from the spin to propel his elbow into his assailant's face. The man's nose broke and the front of his skull caved in, fragments of bone slicing into the brain.

Tomas ripped the dead man's sword from his hands and stabbed it into another mercenary.

Then the fight was truly joined. Tomas' sword sliced into undefended limbs and bodies. The mercenaries had to avoid one another, slowing their own strikes even further. No such restrictions plagued Tomas. There were no friends for him to worry about on the street.

His opponents were too slow, but worse, they were too predictable. Their cuts lacked imagination. They were tough men, well-used to the efficacy of brute force. Against the weak and untrained, their methods had been enough to eke out a living.

None of them would have survived many battles in the war.

Tomas didn't leave any alive long enough to realize the error of their ways. He believed life was a precious gift, but they had forfeited theirs when they volunteered for their task tonight.

He predicted their strikes well before they became reality. Sharp intakes of breath warned him of attacks from behind. Unwashed bodies pressed against him, smelling of ale and sweat.

Dying mercenaries groaned and cursed throughout the street, their corpses and outstretched arms constantly threatening to trip him. But with every exchange another mercenary fell.

Numbers alone didn't tell the story, though. Even against a hundred, only so many can fight a person at once. As more mercenaries fell, the others had to worry less about accidentally cutting their allies.

And those who had survived the initial exchanges were those more skilled with their weapons.

Three attacked at once, each mercenary the point of a constantly shifting triangle with Tomas at its center. When he moved, they followed, the tips of their swords restricting his freedom of movement. If he shifted toward one, the other two would close.

These three had worked together before.

Only the scarred man remained distant. "Who are you?" he asked again. Tomas heard the slight tremor in his voice.

Tomas answered with his sword. He swiped at one of the three swords pointing at him. He put his strength into it, done with this fight. The power of his swing knocked his opponent off his line.

As expected, the other two closed, sensing an opening. But Tomas rushed forward faster than the mercenaries could react. A deep cut to the leg brought down the first point of the triangle. The other two fell in the moments after.

The scarred man retreated as Tomas stepped forward. He didn't plead for mercy, which Tomas appreciated. "You're not even human," he said.

"Not anymore," Tomas agreed.

10

The scarred man attacked.

He possessed true skill. His cuts were precise, his advance measured. And he gave no thought to his own survival.

It was a shame he had accepted Jons' wife's task tonight. Family gold was hardly worth one's life.

Their first pass left a thin cut along the scarred man's neck, a twin to one on the other side of his throat. The second, a deeper one on his leg. The scarred man knew he was bested, but he attacked anyway. The third pass proved fatal.

The mercenary dropped to the ground, bleeding from a deep wound in his side. He held his intestines with his left hand. He groaned softly. Then he looked up at Tomas. "I thought your kind were a myth nowadays."

Tomas shook his head. "The church would have it so."

The mercenary struggled into a kneeling posture. His face was pale and sweat beaded his forehead. "I suppose it's as good a way to go as any." He coughed, blood splattering across the road. He smiled. "I served, too. Same side, I'm guessing."

Tomas nodded.

"Give me a clean death, will you?"

Tomas took up position to the side of the man. The mercenary bowed his head, and Tomas said the old words for the second time that day.

"Thank you," the scarred man said.

Tomas cut, and it was finished. Franz and his family were safe, at least for the night. He drifted over the battlefield, ensuring all were dead. When he was certain, he cleaned off his sword and sheathed it. The fire in his stomach subsided as Elzeth calmed.

He returned to the inn, stripping off the now-bloody uniform.

Franz waited for him in the entryway. The innkeeper's eyes were wide. "I've seen too many battles," he said. "But I've never seen anything like that."

"And with luck, you'll never have to again." Tomas handed him the clothes. "Burn these, now. I'm going to clean up, then return to the gambling hall."

Franz bowed. "I left a basin out next to the garden for you." He paused. "Thank you. I'm not sure what we would have done had you not arrived."

Tomas shook his head. "Don't thank me. But you should leave. This will get worse before it gets better."

Franz grinned. "These old knees don't run the way they used to, I'm afraid." Then he turned and disappeared down the hall.

"He's a fool," Elzeth said.

"I like him," Tomas replied.

"That only proves my point."

They hurried through the inn, exiting out the rear and

into the garden. As Franz had promised, there was water waiting for him. The innkeeper had guessed what was coming. Tomas washed his hands, face, and hair of blood.

When he was certain he was clean, he leaped back over the wall.

The town stirred to life as the sun fell, and the bodies were, of course, starting to attract attention. He didn't bother trying to return the way he had come. He leaped to the rooftops, jumping across them with practiced ease as torches held by curious bystanders gathered in front of the inn.

In the dark, running along the rooftops, Tomas made it quickly back to the hall.

He jumped from the roof across the alley into his room, landing without a sound. He slid the window shut and looked around. As near as he could tell, it was exactly how he'd left it. It was no guarantee someone hadn't come looking for him, but his feeling was that the Family was occupied with other matters. He kneeled and fell into a meditative state.

Before long, familiar footsteps approached his door and there was a gentle knocking. "Come in," Tomas said.

He opened his eyes as Jons slid aside the door. The boss was dressed from head to toe in black, the only splash of color the Family emblem. It was the uniform of the Family when they went to war. It was the uniform they wore when they were buried.

Tomas saw nothing unusual in Jons' expression. He looked like a man on the eve of battle. No suspicion marred his features.

"Is it time?" Tomas asked.

"It is. Tolkin is about to rise," Jons said.

Tomas stood in one smooth motion and followed Jons

down the hallway. Jons didn't seem worried to have Tomas behind him at all. Either trust or distraction stole his attention.

They reached a balcony that overlooked the main gambling hall, and Tomas caught his first look of the assembled might of the Family. He swore.

Jons gave him a tight grin. "The cost is exorbitant, but I do not underestimate the knights."

"You really don't."

The scene below reminded Tomas of a herd of cattle gathered into too small of a corral.

Angry cattle.

Most of them armed.

Jons was playing with fire, but Tomas suspected he already knew well enough.

The boss looked over the assembled gathering as the room quieted. Tomas shifted away from the boss, not wanting to draw extra attention to himself. But even with the additional distance he saw Jons' eyes narrow. "Where's Trenor and his boys?"

The various Family and mercenaries looked around the room, as though they might see something Jons had missed. Near the front door, across the room from Jons, a voice shouted. "They left a while back. Said they had a quick errand to run."

Jons' stare turned cold as ice. His gaze wandered over to his wife, who returned his look without flinching. Tomas didn't think there would ever be forgiveness between those two.

Just then the main door burst open, and nearly a hundred pairs of eyes turned to the front of the hall at the same time. A girl, who barely looked to be of age, entered.

She was out of breath. "Boss! Trenor and his men are all dead! In front of Franz's inn."

"What happened?" Jons asked.

"Watchers told me it was one warrior, from the church."

Several people in the room began muttering about knights.

Tomas focused his attention on Jons. He didn't know the man's whole story, but there was no doubt this moment might very well define his time with the Family. Out of the corner of his eye, he saw Jons' wife lean forward, a vicious smile on her face.

If he backed down, she would call him a coward.

And maybe not today, but someday, he would then lose the Family.

But he'd just lost almost a dozen of his warriors. At least one of whom was skilled. If there was a balance in Jons' head, which way did it now tip?

Tomas couldn't tell. Jons controlled his expression, even as the muttering in the hall grew louder. The sands of time were flowing away. His wife was leaning so far forward, ready to spring into action, Tomas wondered if she might just tip over and fall on her face.

Jons spoke, his voice heavy with confidence. "It is of no matter. We have prepared for more than long enough, and we still have the element of surprise."

His wife returned to a more balanced stance, but Tomas couldn't help but think of a snake, coiled to strike at any moment of perceived weakness. Jons was no ally of his, but Tomas almost felt sorry for him.

Jons continued. "Tonight we fight. Tonight we drive the church from this town for good!"

A familiar energy trickled into the hall. Men and women examined their weapons as instructions were given. Belts were tightened and sheaths adjusted. Friends nodded grimly to one another, or in some cases, embraced. Many went quiet, lost in private worlds.

Tomas recognized the various preparations for battle. The faces now before him were vivid mirrors reflecting the ghosts of his past. Once, he too had readied himself in much the same way, surrounded by men and women far closer to him than his kin had ever been.

Despite the separation he maintained from the other mercenaries, he felt the same energy threatening to suck him in and pull him along. He fought the urge. There was a strength there, the bond of warriors fighting for a common cause, even if that cause was Family gold.

But he was not one of them.

Never again would he fight beside others.

Never again would he watch a friend bleed to death at his side.

But the pull was undeniable. There was something

deeply human about wanting to be part of a group, to be part of something larger than the self.

Even if that group was a motley collection of criminals and cutthroats preparing for battle.

Tomas tried to estimate the Family's chances. Few warriors impressed him at a glance, but in a crowd he couldn't be certain. Even with the loss of the mercenaries earlier in the evening, he had little doubt Jons commanded a far larger force than the church.

But numbers only told part of the story. Eight knights were a powerful force. In fair combat, each knight was worth at least six or seven of the warriors in the hall. They spent their lives training to defend their beliefs and were more than willing to die for them. Few here could claim anything close.

Tomas gave up on his predictions. He didn't know enough about the church's forces, and battles were just as often decided by a twist of fate as they were any skill or planning.

The archer who misses her target but hits a messenger carrying a vital letter.

The swordsman who trips just as he is about to deliver the decisive blow against the enemy commander.

Wherever two tried to kill one another, chance thrived, gambling away lives.

Jons marshaled his forces with surprising efficiency. With so few in the hall being Family, Tomas had expected discipline issues. But he saw none. The mercenaries took their orders and prepared for the fight. Jons must have been paying them well indeed to have them jumping at the sound of his voice.

Tomas remained near the boss as they all streamed out

of the hall. The street was deserted, and Tomas wondered if his warning had been heeded.

The mercenaries formed into small groups of various sizes, clumping with others they were familiar with. Two groups of Family, numbering four each, peeled off from the main advance and onto more residential streets. They represented the whole of Jons' strategy. Ideally, they would flank the knights when the battle began. Tomas wasn't sure what good they would actually accomplish, but he supposed it was a slightly better plan than blindly charging forward.

Jons, to his credit, led his advance from the front. Tomas followed a few paces behind.

Jons walked tall, his pace calm and unhurried. He was the very ideal of the competent commander. He had put to rest whatever doubts might have arisen about him back in the hall.

In contrast, the mercenaries lost their shallow confidence with every step. They resisted, not falling behind, exactly, but putting a little distance between themselves and Jons' honor guard. Glances shot back and forth between friends. No one wanted to be the coward who halted first, but no one pressed to be near the front of the advance.

That was the problem with mercenaries. As much as people desired coin, few valued it more than their own lives. People would sacrifice themselves by the thousands if you told them it was in the name of a higher purpose. But for coin? That was a much harder argument to make.

It was easy to be a mercenary when all you had to do was spend your boss' coin freely and swagger around town like you owned the place. It was harder when marching toward a church knight.

Would Jons' force break?

Tomas couldn't guess. But he was certain they wouldn't fight with the same fire the knights would.

"Regretting your choices?" Elzeth asked.

"Usually."

They passed Franz's inn. Trenor and his men lay there, as dead as Tomas had left them. Then they reached church territory, but still there was no sign of the knights. Tomas tensed.

The knights appeared, emerging from several buildings at once and taking up position in the street. All eight of them. Even if the commander didn't like him, he'd taken the warning seriously.

The formation brought Jons to a stop. His one hope had been to surprise the knights. The boss glanced back, his eyes searching for the traitor among his mercenaries.

Which was the other problem with hired help.

A distinct lack of loyalty.

Tomas had no trouble imagining Jons' predicament. His odds of winning this fight kept decreasing. But to turn around would be labeled cowardice by his wife. His tenuous hold on the Family would slip.

Jons seemed like the type who would choose death before dishonor. In fact, Tomas counted on it.

And he wasn't disappointed.

Jons set his shoulders and drew his sword, adding a dramatic flourish at the end. Against the knights, he'd just eliminated any chance of a peaceful resolution. He pointed his blade at the enemy commander. "This is your last chance to leave this town."

Tomas heard the hint of hope in the boss' voice.

But he had drawn his sword, so there was only one way this would end.

The knight commander drew his own weapon in response.

In the dark of night, the street lit only by the pale reddish glow of Tolkin, dozens of swords were drawn. The knights assumed their traditional stances. Knights tended to fight either alone or in pairs, and here, their positioning indicated they planned on fighting as four pairs.

Tomas wasn't sure he'd be able to get duels against the knights, which complicated his life considerably.

Feet shuffled behind him. Jons' mercenaries were preparing to run.

But would it be at the enemy or away from them?

Jons shouted, "Attack!"

There was a moment, no more than a beat of a heart, when no one moved. The whole fate of the town rested on the edge of a blade, ready to fall one way or the other.

It was a younger woman, one of the Family, who pushed them over the edge. She carried a spear, which she thrust in the air as she charged the knights. And as soon as there was one, there were many.

Tomas held back. The first moments of the fight would be crucial in determining his own actions.

The two sides collided. The Family and their mercenaries were like the waves crashing against the unforgiving rocks of the knights. Tomas saw at least five or six mercenaries fall within the first seconds of the battle. More fell soon after, while the knights remained unharmed.

The difference in skill was even greater than Tomas expected. Jons had hired plenty of bodies, but few were skilled enough to earn their coin and survive this slaughter.

Tomas pushed into the fray. The first knight he came across was older, a man who looked to have seen more than forty summers. As Tomas neared, the knight opened a deep gash across a mercenary's leg. Blood pumped from the wound as the woman fell.

The cut told Tomas all he needed to know about his opponent. The knight's technique was straightforward and efficient. Wasted movement had been stripped from his style over years of disciplined practice.

A dangerous opponent, but not necessarily a creative one.

Like most of the knights.

The knight's partner was close behind. She was small and fast, but at the moment busy with what appeared to be a whole company of mercenaries. Despite being severely outnumbered, she was winning.

But the mercenary lives gave Tomas the time he needed to duel.

The knight saw Tomas approach and turned to meet him.

Tomas cut, but the knight parried. In response, the knight made his own cut, the movement both perfectly executed and predictable.

Tomas slid away, answering with a strike of his own. The knight's eyes widened slightly as he observed Tomas' skill. But he still blocked the attack.

They passed again, the sound of their duel lost amidst the clanging steel and dying groans. The other mercenaries didn't come close, content to let the two masters fight with each other. But the knight's partner had almost finished against the company, and then she would come to help.

Tomas pressed harder, but the knight refused to make a fatal mistake. In time, Tomas would wear him down. A sword was a heavy weapon. But he didn't have time. The other knight was down to her last two opponents.

His limbs grew stronger. His eyes sharper. The once dim light of Tolkin now seemed as bright as the sun at noon.

Tomas advanced, alert to every muscle movement in his opponent. The knight was an incredible swordsman. But he wasn't enough.

It still took Tomas two passes to bring the knight down.

He won just as his partner finished with her bloody work and turned to help.

She saw her partner fall, and in that moment, she lost control. Wearied from her previous fight, she leaped at him with wild swings. With her natural speed and skill, she might have bested most warriors with the move.

But Tomas saw it all, could predict every cut.

With such knowledge, victory was easy. He angled his body and cut just so, and his sword went through her.

She fell, and the knights' strength was suddenly down a quarter.

The Family came from the side streets, flanking the remaining six knights. Tomas felt the tide of the battle begin to turn.

In response, he backed off, allowing the mercenaries to flow around him as they concentrated on the six remaining knights.

Another knight fell, but only after taking many mercenaries with her. The knights were getting pushed together. Spears darted at the church warriors, herding them ever closer.

Tomas wondered if the battle was almost over.

And then thunder echoed in the streets as the church watchtower opened fire.

12

Tomas saw the bullet as it passed over his shoulder. One of the Family behind him fell.

He had the distinct suspicion the shot had been aimed at him.

When another bullet split the air beside him, his suspicion became a certainty. Those in the watchtower had seen him kill the two knights.

Which made him their target of choice.

Tomas ducked, keeping bodies between him and the watchtower.

The rifles changed everything.

The knights knew it, too. They pressed the attack, and the tide of the battle turned again. The Family and their mercenaries lost the ground they had just won, and they were moments from breaking. No one had come prepared for rifles.

Two more shots boomed from the watchtower and two more mercenaries fell. With the bodies so tightly pressed together in the street, the shooters almost couldn't miss.

Jons' forces broke. One step backward became many,

and then backs turned and ran for the safety of the gambling hall.

Tomas hesitated for a moment, then joined them. He had no desire to stand against the knights alone.

Two more shots ended two more lives, the bullets taking the fleeing mercenaries in the back.

Elzeth's anger roared to life, mirrored by Tomas' own. But Tomas restrained himself and remained with the others. Five knights and two rifles were too much, even for him.

The cowardly shooters would receive their just reward, in time.

Tomas glanced back once as they fled. The knights didn't pursue the mob. A few knelt over their dead, and the commander watched Jons' forces run.

Just outside the gambling hall, Jons' wife waited for them. No doubt, she had watched the whole debacle. Warriors poured past her into the perceived safety of the hall. Family and mercenaries alike collapsed into chairs or onto the floor. Few were injured. Most of those who had fought directly with the knights were dead.

Tomas looked around the room. More than half of Jons' forces had been killed. Somewhere between thirty and forty remained. All for three knights.

Jons stood at the door, looking over what remained of his might. His face was ashen.

Perhaps because he'd just lost the town.

Or maybe he felt some guilt over his role in all of this.

Jons' wife marched over to her husband. She kept her voice low, but Tomas used Elzeth to listen in.

"You failed! How could you not know they had guns?" she demanded.

He turned slowly to her. "How *could* I have known,

Mara? We have no informants within the church. Nor do we have any role in supplying them."

"You should have known."

Jons had no further answer to that. Some arguments were impossible to win.

A few wary men and women remained near the windows, watching the street for signs of an attack.

Tomas didn't think one would come. The knights weren't interested in driving the Family from the town. Not yet, at least. If they were, they would have pursued the retreat until every member of the Family was dead. The advantage was firmly theirs, now.

Mara understood that fact, too. Her face was in her husband's, allowing him no escape. "What will you do? You've lost us this town!"

But Jons was somewhere else, his eyes firmly fixed on the future. Tomas saw the way he straightened, as though Mara's anger was a whetstone sharpening his blade. He prepared for the next battle. He hadn't given up.

The same couldn't be said for the mercenaries. As more of them began to realize they wouldn't die tonight, they began to call for liquor, and company.

Tomas' gut clenched.

Tonight would be a wild night.

Few celebrations could equal those after a battle. Won or lost.

Risking death reaffirmed the value of life. The mercenaries would seek to make the most out of the Family's offerings tonight.

Tomas wanted no part of it.

"If the knights attacked now, they could end it all," Elzeth said.

"They won't," Tomas said.

"You think they're protecting it?"

"I do. I don't think they care much about the Family unless they interfere."

Elzeth's thoughts raced. Through their bond, Tomas had some idea of the direction those thoughts took. "So this definitely isn't where we want to be."

Tomas watched Mara still arguing with Jons, now just inside the hall. "Especially not with her wanting to kill us."

"Leave out the back?"

Tomas considered, then gave his head a small shake. "Too many questions. We'll leave out the front."

"She's not going to like that."

"What's she going to do?" Already the party was starting. Alcohol flowed freely. Jons did nothing to slow it. Mara jabbed a finger in his chest, in full sight of everyone. Second by second, control of the Family slid through Jons' grasp.

Tomas started toward the door. No one noticed. A visitor would never guess the magnitude of the defeat that had been handed to the celebrants just minutes ago.

The church might not have to do anything, anyway. This group might end up destroying themselves.

Mara saw him approach, and she stabbed her finger at him like a knife. "And what about him?" she growled. "He killed our son, and you hire him?"

"He killed two knights on his own," Jons replied.

"And that justifies it? Eiro was my son! He was worth more than the whole town put together."

Tomas considered correcting Mara, but decided it wasn't worth the fight. He continued toward the door, but Mara blocked his way.

"Where are you going?" she asked.

"Out."

"There's no way in the three hells I'm letting you leave,"

Mara said. She jabbed her finger into his chest. Jons, having just seen some of Tomas' skill, backed up a step.

Mara didn't notice.

"You do that again," Tomas said, "and you'll regret it."

Something in his tone must have penetrated her grief and anger. She hesitated, but only for a moment. "You'll stay right here."

He didn't flinch. "I know you tried to have me killed tonight. You'll forgive me if I don't trust your offers of hospitality." He slid to the side, intending to step around her and into the street beyond.

She blocked his way again, her earlier hesitation gone. She stabbed the finger into his chest again, some order on her lips.

She never got the first word out. Tomas hit her in the stomach, hard enough to knock the wind out of her. She began to fold over his fist, but he put his other hand on her shoulder to steady her. He pushed her over to Jons.

Tomas stepped into the street and focused on the church watchtower. The pair of watchers remained there, but he saw no rifles. For now, at least, the street was safe. Still, he planned on keeping as many buildings between him and the watchers as he could.

Then he heard the footsteps behind him and the sound of a knife being drawn from its sheath.

Last Sword in the West

13

Tomas turned to see Mara, knife in hand, her whole body trembling in anger. She stepped at him, the motion half an attack, half an attempt to keep him from leaving.

Tomas slapped the knife from her hand dismissively.

She uttered a cry, strangled and broken.

Jons grabbed her by her upper arm, holding her back. Worry flashed in his gaze. "Dear, he killed two knights on his own."

For the first time, Tomas heard affection in Jons' voice. A hint of the love that had once bloomed between them.

Maybe it was that affection in his voice, or perhaps it was the simple repetition of the fact, but this time the news penetrated Mara's thoughts. Her eyes went wide and she took a halting step back, into Jons' waiting arms.

Tomas saw what neither of them could. Behind the couple, within the hall, the eyes of every survivor were upon them. Sellsword and Family alike watched as the most powerful couple in town acquiesced to the stranger.

But they also saw Jons and Mara together. Acting as one for the first time in a long time.

Hopefully, it sucked some of the venom from the wounds Mara had inflicted. Tomas had no love for the Family, but having two forces vying for control of the town made his life easier, his own goals more attainable. The duel between church and Family was rife with opportunity. If the Family collapsed too soon, it made his own tasks more difficult.

Time would tell. He gave the couple a short bow. "If you expect another fight against the knights, let me know, and I shall assist."

Then he turned back to the street.

This time, no one attacked.

The street, all the way to the other side of town, was free of living souls. The knights had retreated to their mission, and no citizen dared leave their home.

Tomas looked up at Tolkin, pale red and swollen with the spirits of the dead. He imagined himself on that far-away surface, looking down on all of this. It seemed such a waste. Even if the church was here for a nexus, surely it wasn't worth so many lives.

Nothing could be.

He sighed and walked back to Franz's inn.

As he neared the battlefield, he paused to observe the result. For all the death, there had been little property damage. The fight had been contained to the street surrounding the knights. The knights had already removed their dead, but the merce-naries and Family still lay where they fell. Tomas wondered, just for a second, how Jons would clean this mess up. Because he claimed this town as his, so the mess was his as well.

Tomas shook his head.

He felt the eyes of the watchers up in the tower. But they made no move for the rifles he now knew were hidden there.

Exhaustion finally hit. He blinked and yawned, then entered Franz's inn. Despite the violence the entryway had suffered from Eiro, there was still a sense of peace within. Tomas breathed easier as he took off his boots and cleaned his face and hands. He went to the dining room, where Franz shared some of what he had cooked for his family that evening.

The food was simple but deeply satisfying. Tomas ate quickly and in silence. Like the excellent host he was, Franz recognized Tomas' mood and left him alone. When he finished the meal he bowed deeply to the old man, climbed the stairs to his room, and fell asleep even as he fell toward his bed.

He woke to the smells of breakfast floating in to his room on currents of warm air.

He ran through a single form, then made himself presentable and went downstairs.

Franz brought a bowl laden with food to Tomas even as he found a table. "Morning," he said.

Tomas pointed at the bowl. "Please tell me that's for me."

Franz nodded. "And plenty more where that came from, if you need."

Tomas' grin stretched across his face and he dug in.

It wasn't long before Franz was bringing a second bowl. "May I join you?" he asked.

"Of course."

The innkeeper needed a few minutes to work up his courage, but Tomas didn't mind. As always, Franz's meals were among the best he could remember eating. It was simple food, but prepared to perfection, and without pretense. Tomas wouldn't miss this town when he left, but he would mourn the loss of these meals.

"What's happening in my town?" Franz finally asked. "Once, this was a good place to live. Perhaps a bit rough around the edges, but filled with neighbors who cared. It could be again, if not for the church and the Family. But I don't understand what they're fighting over. There's nothing here."

"That's where you're wrong," Tomas said.

Franz waited for him to explain.

Tomas finished the second bowl of food. "I'm willing to answer your questions, at least with my best guesses. But you should probably know that everything I'm about to tell you is considered heresy by the church. Even a whisper of it will bring a knight to your door with their sword drawn."

Franz glared. "We still follow the true path. Surely you've figured that out by now."

"Not the same, friend. This will truly get you killed."

Franz shrugged. "I'll keep it quiet, but the church doesn't scare me."

"That makes one of us." Tomas considered asking for a third bowl, then thought better of it. He wouldn't be able to move all day if he ate more. He took a deep breath. "I believe the church and the Family are after something called a nexus. I think there is one here, or nearby."

"A nexus? What's that?"

Tomas grimaced. "Honestly, I'm not quite sure. They are places around the planet where power gathers. They have something to do with the sagani, but I couldn't say what, exactly."

"And this nexus is so important it requires eight knights?"

"The church seems to think so. They seek to control them at all costs, but again, to what end I couldn't say."

"And now the Family wants in, too?"

"That's my guess."

"And you? Is that why you're here, too?"

Tomas shook his head. "I spoke true. My appearance here is nothing more than coincidence. But I have a feeling humans aren't meant to control the nexuses at all."

"So you would turn your blade against everyone?"

Tomas raised an eyebrow. "My intent was to travel west until the problems of the world were behind me. I didn't seek any more fights."

Franz chuckled. "How did that go for you?"

"It hasn't been my best plan so far."

Franz laughed outright at that, and Tomas relaxed. He worried telling the innkeeper so much put him in danger, but Franz was in danger as long as he lived in this town. The Family had a long memory, and would never forget Eiro. Eventually, the laughter subsided. "So, what will you do next?"

"I need to find the nexus. Then I can try to figure out why so many people are willing to fight over them. Hopefully before more die."

The innkeeper nodded. "In that case, I might know exactly where you should start your search."

14

"**I** think he lied," Elzeth said.

Tomas let his eyes wander the horizon. Empty grasslands stretched as far as he could see, with little more than the occasional small copse of trees to break the view. "His directions could have been better," Tomas admitted.

Elzeth laughed. "He gave you a direction and a rough distance. I'm not even sure that qualifies."

"Turn around?"

Elzeth thought for a moment. "Might as well keep exploring for a bit. We're already out here."

Tomas grinned. Elzeth would never say so, of course, but he was just as curious as Tomas. Everything they thought they knew about nexuses was secondhand or worse, an echo of a whisper someone had once heard. Unbelievable stories, half-remembered legends, and drunk confessions of priests served as their guide. Tomas didn't believe any single source was reliable. But when he took all the bits and pieces and mixed them together, there was *something*, a truth at the edge of his understanding.

Elzeth agreed. He couldn't summon memories at will of his time before Tomas. As near as either of them could guess, it was only after their union that Elzeth had developed conscious thought as Tomas recognized it. Every so often they would experience a flash of a time before, a scene not of Tomas' life. But they seemed random, and only came when the barrier between them dissolved.

If forced to describe Elzeth's earlier experiences of the world, Tomas would call them open. A complete awareness, but devoid of thought.

As they collected stories and rumors, Elzeth's interest grew. Of the two of them, he was probably the most obsessed with answers. The nexuses and the sagani had a connection, but it was as mysterious as everything else surrounding the secret places.

So they continued to wander the grasslands. Franz had told them they would know the spot when they saw it. Back at the inn, his caginess had been a mystery, adding an edge of excitement to their search. Now Tomas was wishing he had insisted on a more detailed description of the location.

Elzeth noticed the absence first. "There's not much game around."

The observation stopped Tomas in his tracks. He searched his memory. They'd seen some rabbits and pheasant not too far out of town, but Elzeth was right. They hadn't seen any other wildlife for a while.

"Sagani?" Tomas asked.

"I haven't seen anything, but that doesn't mean much."

"You'd think Franz would have mentioned something."

"If it is a sagani, it's probably adept at avoiding humans. And if it scared off all the game there wouldn't be much reason for humans to be out this way. They might not even know."

"Even more true if the church has been sending knights out this way. I suspect most townspeople wouldn't want to be caught in the wild alone against one or two zealots."

Elzeth agreed. "Might mean we're getting close, though."

Tomas felt a wave of energy as Elzeth woke further.

"Careful," Tomas cautioned. "We haven't even spotted anything yet."

"And by the time you would on your own it will be too late."

Not long after, Tomas swore as he heard the grass parting softly behind him. If not for Elzeth's assistance, he wouldn't have heard the sound.

"Told you," Elzeth smirked.

In this case, Tomas wasn't upset about being wrong. He much preferred being alive than right. He turned, wondering what he would find.

The sagani rose from the grass, growing in size as it did. It stood on two thick legs, and its wide and muscular body was covered in black fur. Four arms ended in meaty paws with claws as long as a knife and as sharp as Tomas' sword. The creature reminded Tomas of the few remaining black bears that still haunted the remotest parts of the mountains out east.

It was just far larger, and with an extra set of arms.

The sagani roared, the power of the sound forcing Tomas back a step. Then it swiped at Tomas, who dove to the side.

He didn't draw his sword, but he didn't retreat, either. Both plans most likely ended with him bleeding to death in the middle of nowhere. Instead, he stood tall as the creature came at him again.

Elzeth responded for both of them. He burned within Tomas, threatening to bring him down to a knee.

But Tomas found the strength to stand.

The sagani paused, then dropped down onto all six paws. It came closer, sniffing at Tomas.

He fought the desire to reach for his sword. Though the sagani looked like a lumbering bear, Tomas expected it could strike as quick as a diving falcon. This close, Tomas wasn't sure he had any chance of defending himself.

Elzeth spoke.

At least, that was how Tomas described it. The action wasn't like when the two of them spoke. That was a conversation in his head, two distinct human voices no one else could hear. This was sound and movement, like a dance, but at the very limits of human perception.

The sagani watched them, responding in the same manner, though to Tomas' eye the creature stood still. The contradictions between perception and observation threatened to shatter his mind, but he had enough experience with Elzeth to know he needed to relax. Paradox was a normal part of existence, only a problem when logic demanded satisfaction. The world didn't work the way humans thought it did.

The sooner they learned that, the better off they would all be.

The sagani spoke without sound and danced without moving. Tomas couldn't explain the mysteries, but he didn't feel the need to.

Elzeth had taught him how to be open to possibility.

And after a few minutes, the bear-shaped creature turned away and shrunk until it was almost invisible in the grass.

"Follow her," Elzeth said. When Tomas took a step, he added, "at a distance, maybe."

Tomas thought that piece of advice wise.

Even knowing it was ahead, Tomas needed to focus to track the sagani. It barely left a ripple in the grass as it walked. Without sharpened senses, the task would have been next to impossible.

They walked for about a mile, then Tomas felt a deep unease. The sagani cried, an inaudible lament that tore at his heart. A cry for something lost. The creature shrank even further, now no larger than a field mouse. It scurried away and Tomas lost it.

"It was warning us," Elzeth said. "Of what, I'm not sure."

Tomas nodded. A rise in the land was before them, and he walked up it, remaining low. As he neared the crest, he dropped to hands and knees and crawled forward.

The nexus was there. A small pond, no more than a few hundred feet wide. But it had depth, its waters dark. Trees surrounded the water.

Tomas tore his attention away from the pond to take in the area. Everything in front of him seemed out of place, as though a different geology had been lifted from somewhere else and placed here. Ponds in the grasslands were typically shallow affairs, depressions that had filled in with water. And the pond and the trees were surrounded on all sides by a rise in the land, like a crater.

It didn't make sense, yet it was.

Tomas accepted the addition of yet another mystery into his life.

Movement caught his eye. He focused on it and saw the barrel of a rifle on the rise about two hundred feet to his left. The owner of the rifle was concealed by a blind. A good one, too. Tomas suspected most of it was dug into the ground.

He ignored it for now. Thanks to the sagani's warning, he'd arrived without being noticed. The rifle prevented him from nearing the nexus, but there was no hurry.

Tomas examined the area again. The grass, trees, and even the water seemed more vivid, more alive.

But the nexus wasn't anything like he expected. What was it about this place that was worth so many lives?

After watching for a few minutes, Tomas retreated until he was on the other side of the rise. Though he was only a few hundred feet from the nexus, it was now hidden from view. He stood and stretched. The day was getting late, so he began the walk back to town. The thought of another one of Franz's meals put a spring in his step.

Two miles later, he came to a complete stop.

Banners waved lazily in the evening breeze, and tents were being erected. Tomas watched as outriders rode toward him.

"Didn't think I'd see this anytime again," Elzeth said.

"Me neither."

Tomas waited for the outriders to reach him, studying the activity ahead of him. He laughed. Jons would probably be delighted, but the commander of the knights would quietly rage.

Tomas didn't know what an army was doing out here, but the situation in Franz's small town had just gotten much more complicated.

15

The riders came to a halt a dozen paces away from him. Wary but relaxed, they offered short bows that Tomas returned. "Well met," one said.

"Indeed," Tomas replied. Closer now, he could read the insignia on their uniforms. "What brings the 34th out this way?"

"Training exercise, and a long one. You a soldier?"

"Once."

"What are you doing out here?"

"Traveling west. There's a town nearby with a great inn. Been resting there for a couple of days, but wanted to explore a bit today."

"West, eh?" The rider looked out that way. "Any particular destination?"

"As far as my legs will carry me."

The rider nodded. He looked old enough to have served in the war. His manner spoke of a veteran. He understood. "Our commander would probably like a word, if you'd be willing."

He had the manners to phrase it as a request, but it was

an order all the same. Tomas nodded and followed the two riders as they rode slowly into camp.

Tomas knew several units had been ordered west after the war, and had heard rumors that a few had even made it this far. But he was still surprised. He wasn't that far from the edge of known territory. Feeding and moving an army was no small feat, which meant they tended to stay close to populated areas where they could more easily supply.

If they were this far west, they were here for a reason.

And it wasn't a training exercise.

Guard dogs barked at his arrival, but they were quieted by their masters. There were few better protections out here in the wild. Dogs could smell a sagani quite a distance away, providing invaluable early warnings to soldiers. Unfortunately, it also meant the dogs didn't like him much. His scent tended to confuse them.

They paused near the edge of camp, where the riders passed their horses off to a stable master. Then they escorted Tomas further in.

Everywhere he looked, Tomas saw soldiers setting up camp with practiced efficiency. No one rushed, but he didn't see anyone lazing around, either. Truth be told, it was one of the more organized camps he'd ever seen. He'd never fought the 34th in his own service, but he suspected they were formidable.

The sights and sounds unearthed memories Tomas had worked hard to bury. He'd spent no small number of nights in camps just like this one. Though he'd barely ever been part of a unit like this, his small band had often camped with larger forces, and even though they were often strangers, they had always been welcomed.

A part of him longed for those nights again. Though the memories were now tainted by tragedy, he'd once lived for quiet evenings around campfires, swapping stories with the regulars and getting drunk on whatever piss passed for alcohol in the camp.

As a soldier, he'd once been part of something bigger than himself.

And though he'd never return to the life of a soldier, he missed that.

The riders brought him to a tent barely larger than any other. "We'll need your sword."

Tomas shook his head. "That request I must refuse. I'm sorry."

The riders shared a glance and one went into the tent. Tomas could hear the conversation within, though he gave no indication of it. A moment later, the rider exited and nodded. "He doesn't mind."

They escorted Tomas in and took positions near the entrance.

The commander squatted near the center of the tent, where a small fire had been built and a pot of water was boiling. He glanced up at his guest.

"Welcome," he said, his voice deep and strong. "Please, allow your sword to rest next to mine." He gestured over to the side, where a simple wooden rack held a single sword.

Tomas bowed, removed his sword, and placed it on the rack, in the bottom empty space. By the time he finished, the commander was kneeling beside the fire. Tomas knelt down across from him.

"Would you join me for a cup of tea?" the commander asked. "It's a small ritual I enjoy after a day of travel."

"I'd be honored," Tomas said.

The commander's hair appeared to have turned gray long ago, but he didn't seem that old to Tomas. Fifty, at the most. And he moved with the grace and strength of a younger man. His actions were smooth and deliberate, his hands steady.

Formidable, indeed. Tomas better understood the efficiency of the camp now.

"I'm General Gaven of the 34th," he said as he poured the tea. "It's a pleasure to meet you."

Tomas bowed. "Tomas, and likewise."

"You move like a warrior."

"Once, perhaps, but my war is behind me."

The general picked up his tea and took a sip. Tomas did the same. It was good. Fragrant and grassy, with just a hint of sweetness that lingered on the tongue.

"Do you really believe so?" Gaven asked.

Tomas blinked.

"That your war is behind you? I've been stationed out west for two years now, and in that time we've come across countless warriors. Many are running, but few seem to have escaped. Are you one of the few?"

Tomas sipped at his tea as he thought. Then he shook his head. "Not yet."

"What unit did you serve with?"

"The 110th." Not the truth, but the truth might get him killed. And he'd spent enough time around the 110th he could answer any questions.

"They fought well. Not many survived the Battle of Krist, though."

Tomas had been there. He remembered.

Some hint of it must have passed over his face. "I'm sorry to bring up the memories," Gaven said. "Why are you out here?"

Tomas repeated the explanation he'd given the riders.

Gaven nodded to the riders, and they exited the tent.

Apparently, they all believed Tomas wasn't much of a threat. "What do you hope to find?"

"Nothing," Tomas said. "As much nothing as I can."

Gaven slowly spun his tea cup in his hands. "You're not the first who has said as much. But not many make it. People need other people."

"Perhaps. But I've spent my whole life in the east, and I've seen the first hints of the future. It's not for me."

"In that, we agree," Gaven said. "I was delighted when I received my orders to come west."

"Why *are* you here?"

"Training maneuvers," the general answered.

"That's nonsense," Tomas said. A rude comment, but he felt a certain kinship with the general and thought it would pass.

It did. Gaven nodded. "It's an open secret. We *are* on training maneuvers, but that isn't our true purpose. We're actually mapping out the area. Detailed maps, along with pages and pages of information on resources."

"Why bring an army for mapping?"

Gaven chuckled grimly. "Because a surprising number of explorers we send out west never return."

"Really?"

"It can't be that much of a surprise. There are the dangers of the wild, of course, but no resource is more valuable than land. The Family, the church, the government, and more all have their eyes on it. And some are already staking their claim." As the general spoke, his eyes never left Tomas. "So, my orders are to explore this land and create the most accurate maps I can."

"How long will you be out?"

"We're actually on our way back to Tansai. Our expedition, for now, is coming to a close."

Tomas nodded, an idea forming in his mind. "Would you say there is no affection, then, between the 34th, the Family, and the church?"

Gaven leaned forward, curious. "None at all."

Tomas smiled. "Then I know just the place your army should visit next. Even better, the food is delicious."

16

Tomas woke up in a familiar, comfortable bed. He yawned and stretched, then smiled as he came to his feet and looked out the window of his room. As usual, the town was quiet in the morning, but it wasn't because the streets were empty.

Members of the 34th walked up and down the town, never in less than pairs. They visited shops and spoke kindly with those they passed. They were unfailingly polite. Even in town, their rigid discipline held.

Tomas went through a few of his forms, careful to step lightly. Then he visited the inn's baths. No longer did he have the place to himself. Many of Gaven's ranking officers boarded at Franz's inn, and a rotating handful of soldiers slept in the bunks downstairs every night. Franz and his family could be found everywhere. No matter the hour, they always seemed to be cooking, cleaning, or otherwise serving. Franz beamed from ear to ear whenever Tomas saw him.

No doubt it was the most they had earned in some time, but Tomas suspected Franz's joy went deeper than that. He wasn't just an innkeeper. He was a born host, and a host without guests was a ship without a sea to sail on. For the first time in their brief acquaintance, Franz seemed truly alive.

Tomas bowed to the others in the bath, enduring the cheers offered in his name. All the soldiers knew he was the one who had led them here, and with a solid month of travel still before them, they were glad for the respite from the hard living on the trail.

He bathed quickly, broke his fast, and went out into the streets of the town. Then he began his own rounds.

The side of town the Family ran was by far the busier of the two. Most of the shops were here, and with the arrival of the army, the shopkeepers had found a reason to open before noon. The difference between the town four days ago and today was so stark it still made Tomas chuckle.

It was a farce, and everyone knew it. But there was no evidence of wrongdoing, so everyone went around as if this town was no different than any other.

Somehow, Jons had cleaned up the town before the army arrived. No doubt, vast sums of gold had been parted with to convince the mercenaries to help with the removal of the bodies. Tomas didn't know where the corpses had been buried, but didn't much care, either. The church burned the bodies of believers, and Tomas suspected Jons had burned those on his side, too. Not out of religious obligation, but the need to hide evidence.

Burned and buried.

A common end for those who dealt with the Family.

Now the Family-owned businesses served the soldiers, smiling and pretending everything was fine. Quite a number of the mercenaries had also been pressed into service, and the sight of a scarred warrior peeling potatoes in a kitchen had almost been too funny for Tomas to stand.

It couldn't last.

Without evidence of some rather heinous crime, Gaven and the 34th would continue on. They would be expected in Tansai before long, and their mission wasn't to keep the peace out here. But their presence bought Tomas time.

He bowed at several shop owners as he passed, ignoring the scowls he saw from Family loyalists.

"You know once Gaven leaves, everyone in this town will want to kill you." Elzeth's tone was as dry as the autumn air.

"At least they have one thing they can agree on."

"You should follow your own advice to Franz and leave before that happens."

Elzeth wasn't making light of the situation. They'd talked often since their return from the nexus. Neither of them wanted to abandon the nexus to the church, but with their lack of knowledge, they didn't know how to proceed. They didn't even know what, exactly, they were trying to prevent the church from accomplishing. Tomas just knew the church wanted the nexus, and that was reason enough to interfere.

On the first day after the army had arrived, Tomas had tried to leave to see the nexus again but was stopped. Gaven had locked down all travel to and from the town, an injunction that applied to Tomas as well.

At most, Tomas figured he had a few more days. A few more days before the army left, and then maybe another day as both sides ensured Gaven and his soldiers were gone. Tomas turned and walked down a residential street, making his way to the other side of town.

The church-controlled side was far more quiet. Soldiers strolled here, but there was little to hold their attention. The church mission left its doors open, inviting the soldiers within, but few gave the mission more than a passing glance.

Tomas turned back onto the main street.

The knight commander came out of a building in front of him. The man started when he noticed Tomas.

They hadn't seen each other since the night of the battle.

The commander's hand went to his sword, but then his eyes took in the number of soldiers walking up and down the street and he stopped. He did walk directly toward Tomas, though. "I'm surprised you're still in town," he said.

Tomas shrugged. "It's a nice place. And with such friendly people."

He almost wanted the commander to attack.

Unfortunately, Tomas was almost as limited in his choices as the Family and knights were. He didn't want the attention of the army, either. From what he'd seen, he could kill the knight commander in a duel, but then he'd have all of the 34th to deal with. Even he wasn't that good.

But he failed to get a further rise out of the knight. The commander shook his head. "You don't have many friends left. Mara still wants you dead for what you did to her son, and there's quite a few Family who agree with her. And you've killed two knights, which means the church will hunt you even if you do try to flee. So what will you do?"

Tomas ignored the question. "Why are so many knights here?"

The commander opened his arms out wide, as though he was embracing the entire town. "We're here to save everyone, to spread the word of the holy church in the dark wilds of the west." Then his smile grew wider as he backed up a couple of steps. "Do you have any desire to confess or repent?"

Tomas shook his head.

"That's a shame. Whispers have reached me that the Family has requested special aid from Tansai. My sources couldn't get too many details, but it sounds as if they are bringing in one of their strongest warriors. Something of a legendary assassin, in fact."

"Then shouldn't you be more worried?"

The commander laughed. "I look forward to our inevitable conflict. But apparently the knights aren't the assassin's primary target." He turned away and spoke over his shoulder.

"You are."

17

Tomas stood in the street outside Jons' gambling hall, debating the wisdom of his plan.

"It's a terrible plan," Elzeth said.

"It's too good of an offer. He'll have to take it."

"*If* Mara hasn't convinced everyone inside, including her husband, that you'd be better off cut into little pieces, scattered to the four winds."

That was a good point. "They wouldn't dare. Not with the army here."

"Sure, they won't kill you in public," Elzeth agreed. "But you're walking straight into the middle of their operation! You're like a pig who just happened to throw yourself onto a spit over a nicely stoked fire."

"You're getting nervous in your old age."

Still, he remained outside, where there were plenty of soldiers to keep him company. Elzeth wasn't wrong. Even though there were almost certainly a handful of off-duty soldiers inside the gambling hall, it was the heart of hostile territory. A foolish man, like him, could find plenty of ways to end up uncomfortably dead. Ways that his new soldier friends wouldn't even notice.

But Tomas didn't like the idea of avoiding Jons.

There were only two ways of handling conflict.

The first was to avoid it completely. Run away, into another town. Or even another country at this point. Tomas preferred that method. He was good at it, thanks to years of practice. But Franz and his cursed stubbornness prevented him. If he ran, he'd only be signing the family's death sentences. Which left only the second way. Attack the problem directly until it wasn't a problem anymore.

Tomas stepped into the hall, ignoring the two Family guarding the door. They made no effort to stop him.

The mood inside the hall was subdued. No small number of the surviving mercenaries had been pressed into service as staff. The sight of them immediately justified Tomas' decision to enter. He chuckled to himself. One giant mercenary, who looked practically naked without his enormous war hammer in his hands, was trying to sweep the floor. Another cutthroat who really didn't appear to understand the concept of bathing scrubbed at a table. The number of "staff" wildly outnumbered the few soldiers playing cards at a pair of tables.

Jons had to be gushing money like blood from an arterial cut.

Tomas couldn't imagine anyone believed the deception. The staff looked so angry they were as likely to slit a throat as serve a drink, and Tomas didn't think he'd ever been in any establishment with so many staff and so few customers.

But they all played the game. If someone in the Family, or one of their mercenaries, slipped up badly enough, Gaven would have reason to intervene. And the general had the strength to break the Family over his knee. The mercenaries would lose the coin they'd worked so hard to earn, as well as their freedom to wander these lands and do as they pleased.

All eyes turned to him as he entered. The soldiers, recognizing him, waved and smiled. The mercenaries and Family scowled at him. Tomas ignored them all, making a straight line for Jons, who sat by himself at the bar.

Jons turned a cold eye on him, but otherwise made no move.

Tomas sat on the stool next to the boss. He couldn't help himself. "Been pretty quiet around here lately. Your mercenaries seem like they appreciate the new work."

He didn't get a rise out of Jons. Not that he'd expected to. He wasn't sure the man had many emotions to manipulate.

"A wise man," Jons said, "wouldn't choose to make an enemy of me."

"I saw a chance to give you time. Your position was weakened after the battle."

Jons took a short sip of his drink. "I was surprised to find out you'd been out in the grasslands. Given my wife's anger toward Inaya and her role in this mess, I didn't expect you to leave the inn. You care for them."

The boss was fishing. Jons suspected something about Tomas was amiss. Not that Tomas sought to betray him. That was a given. Out here, if you weren't with the Family, the church, or the army, you were for yourself. Jons had always known that. Work together long enough and eventually betrayal becomes inevitable.

No, this was worse. He suspected what Tomas was. He wanted to know for sure.

"I'll admit I have a soft spot for Franz," Tomas said. "He serves the best food I've eaten since I started journeying west."

"Sure it isn't the daughter?" Jons asked. "Every man in town wants her as a wife. Even the married ones."

The statement was designed to provoke, but Jons wasn't the only one who could control his emotions. Tomas looked over to the boss. "A wise man," he said, "would choose to leave that family alone. And a very wise man would know better than to threaten that girl."

Jons finished his drink. "Why are you here?"

"I need your help. I want to leave town."

"You should have thought of that before inviting the 34th to visit."

"Perhaps. I didn't expect General Gaven to be quite so vigorous in his protection of the town."

Jons signaled for another drink. "And why are you suddenly so interested in leaving town?"

"Noticed a few people from the church out on my earlier walk. Figured I would go say hello."

Jons' drink arrived and he took another sip. "I'm getting the impression you don't like the church much."

"Can't say I do."

Jons twirled the alcohol in his glass. "Lost a few friends to the knights, did you?"

Tomas didn't answer. It would have been as good as confessing what he was.

Jons twirled the drink some more, staring off into the distance. Tomas was betting than Jons would believe the benefit was worth the risk. If he was also after the nexus, having Tomas take out the defenders would simplify his life considerably. Without church snipers, he could waltz in and control the area.

Jons nodded. "Be here tonight, at dusk. I've got a way out."

Tomas stood and offered a slight bow of his head.

"Thank you."

He turned away, halfway expecting a knife in his back.

It didn't come.

But he knew it would later, after he had lost any usefulness to the boss.

TOMAS RETURNED to the hall that night as directed. He'd rested at Franz's inn, suspecting it might be a while before he got to sleep in a nice comfortable bed again. Franz had filled his stomach once more, a worried look in his eye as he took Tomas' dishes away.

The gambling hall was only slightly busier than it had been earlier that day, a sure sign that life in this town had changed. Again, the primary customers appeared to be the soldiers of the 34th. But even in their gambling, they were disciplined. There would be no rowdy fights, no drunken insults among this group.

He wondered how long it would be before Gaven gave up trying to find evidence of wrongdoing in town.

Jons met him on the main floor and led him through the kitchen and out the back door. Tomas found himself in the same alley that he'd used to sneak away from the hall a couple of days ago.

It wasn't empty today. Two enormous draft horses stomped their feet, eager to be off. Behind them was one of the larger carts Tomas had recently come across. It had to be seven feet wide and ten long, and it was built sturdy enough to carry the draft horses who pulled it.

Jons motioned him toward the cart. The boss nodded at one of his men, who pried some boards from the bottom of the cart, revealing a false bottom. Tomas looked around. "Really?"

"It's a tight fit, but you aren't the first person we've had to smuggle across a line," Jons replied. "They'll get you past the line, then let you out. You'll have to find your way back in."

Tomas grimaced, but climbed into the cart and slid into the false bottom. The boards were placed back over him, brushing against his chest. He calmed his breath. He hated tight spaces.

Then something heavy was placed on top of the boards, causing them to bend a little. He had to work to breathe.

He focused on nothing but his breath. Easy in, easy out. His body cried for more air, but it would have to wait.

The cart rumbled forward. The movement of the cart and the cargo combined to make breathing even more difficult. He worried he'd need Elzeth's strength just to keep air flowing into his lungs.

Elzeth seemed entertained by the idea. "After all the fights you've seen, you're going to be terribly embarrassed when you die from asphyxiation in a smuggler's compartment."

Tomas almost laughed, but immediately regretted it. He returned his focus to his breath.

Before long, the cart came to a stop. Tomas didn't need Elzeth's help to hear the conversation.

"You know no one is allowed to leave," said a woman's voice.

"We're taking it to your camp. Orders from the boss. He says it's a gift for your service to the country."

Footsteps circled the cart, and it shook as someone jumped in. The weight on top of Tomas shifted, and his breath came easier. Then whoever had climbed on jumped down.

"Very well," the woman said. "But be back here within

the hour. Otherwise our fastest riders are coming after you, and they won't ask any questions."

"Yes, ma'am."

The cart continued forward, bringing Tomas that much closer to his next battle.

18

Tomas gulped at the fresh air when the boards were removed. The man who'd freed Tomas chuckled. "A little tight?"

Tomas sat up, still enjoying the sensation of full lungs. "Just a bit."

"Better hurry, the guard didn't give us much time to drop this off and get back."

Tomas saw a barrel of wine next to him and then understood how they'd gotten through the line. Alcohol, perhaps an army's greatest weakness.

Obeying the Family, though, Tomas stretched his legs and dropped from the cart. He offered his guides a short bow, and without further discussion, was off.

He jogged away from the cart toward the nexus, a relatively slow pace that he could maintain for hours. For the first mile, he kept his eyes and ears open for patrols from the 34th. Fortunately, he didn't encounter any and was able to make good time.

At his pace it only took about an hour to bring the rise into view. As soon as it did, Tomas stopped and crouched in the grass. He caught his breath as he watched the lip of the rise. To his sharpened senses, he appeared to be alone, but the hairs on the back of his neck stood straight up.

"Slow or fast?" Elzeth asked.

Tomas bit his lower lip. He'd been wondering the same. "Slow," he decided.

Elzeth settled, and Tomas began the long process of covering the last half mile of ground to the rise. He walked for a while, finding a dip in the land that cut off line of sight from the rise. But before long he was crouching and then crawling.

He paced himself, crawling fifty to a hundred feet at a time, then taking a break.

The breeze blew above him, but down in the grasses, sweat dripped from his face. Even at a gentle pace, crawling was considerably harder than walking. During his breaks he watched the rise, but he still saw nothing.

His unease remained. Someone was there, watching the approaches. If Tomas had to guess, they watched with a rifle in hand. The church seemed to have a few of the weapons out here. Combined with the knights, they'd really spared no expense.

More than once, Tomas reconsidered his slow approach. Crawling gave him the opportunity to surprise the church defenders, but if he was spotted first, it was likely a bullet would find him before he even realized he'd failed.

But he didn't know enough about the defenses the church had in place. He'd only spotted the one blind on his last visit, but he wasn't confident enough to say for certain it was the only defense in the area. If he rushed in, that lack of knowledge might just be what killed him.

And so he crawled, reducing the distance to the rise a couple of dozen paces at a time.

Eventually, when both moons were high in the sky, he reached the bottom of the rise.

Above him, someone coughed.

They'd covered their mouth and muffled the noise, but the sound was unmistakable. Tomas still couldn't see them, but he'd been right to worry. And now he knew approximately where one of the defenders lay.

He crawled slowly, gently parting the grass with his hand before shifting his weight forward. When the breeze gusted overhead he risked moving a little faster.

Elzeth sharpened his hearing.

The man's breathing was soft and even.

And close.

Tomas continued crawling, passing within twenty feet of the man.

He circled behind, each movement carefully planned in advance. He drew a knife from a hidden sheath, then crawled forward, moving one limb at a time.

A strong breeze came up, swishing the tops of the grass in rough circles. Then the wind vanished and it was silent.

The perfect quiet made Tomas' ears burn as they strained for clues. He couldn't even hear the man's breath. He tensed.

Something had alerted the sniper. Perhaps a sound, or even a scent. Maybe a sixth sense, the same type that had warned Tomas that the empty grasslands were not as quiet as they seemed.

The man finished exhaling, and Tomas welcomed the sound. But the sniper suspected. Tomas heard it in the man's breath, which came faster now.

This was no random parishioner, given a rifle and a place to guard. The man might not be a knight, but he was a veteran all the same.

Tomas guessed he was about five or six feet away. He still couldn't see the man. The grass was too thick.

"Now," he said to Elzeth.

The sagani flared to awareness within him. Tomas sprinted forward, staying low, covering the last few paces to the marksman in an instant.

The man barely had time to react. He had been lying prone and was just starting to turn over when Tomas reached him.

Tomas drove the blade of his knife into the man's back, between the ribs and into the heart. A difficult spot to hit well, but with Tomas' senses sharpened, the man moved too slow.

Tomas clapped his free hand over the man's mouth, but there was no need. The life went out of his eyes and he flopped back into the prone position.

Elzeth quieted himself without having to be asked. Tomas took a few deep breaths, gently shaking the sudden energy out of his limbs. Then he looked over the area. The rifleman had chosen his placement well. He'd been in the center of a tall, thick clump of grasses that provided excellent cover. Lying prone, he'd had a clear view of most approaches to the rise, or at least, those that came from the town.

Tomas examined the rifle the man had held. He didn't know the weapons well, but this one looked both new and well cared for. Franz would have had to work for years to earn enough to purchase this weapon, if anyone was even willing to sell to him. And the church had brought several.

Tomas turned the man over and studied him. He was tall and thin, with a full beard covering a weathered face. Old enough to have served, which meant he was yet another wanderer out in the west, one who had chosen to side with the church. Given the local knight commander's attitude, it was probably safe to assume the marksman was a believer, not a mercenary.

Tomas created a story. A veteran, lost after the war as so many were. Traveled the land out west, probably for a few years, given his build. Something had led him to the church, a place where he was welcomed and given a chance to serve once again.

Tomas' stomach twisted.

A waste.

The veteran had chosen wrong.

There was little else to see. The man had some dried meat nearby as well as a canteen. The water was still pretty full, which implied the man hadn't been on watch all that long.

Tomas sighed. One warrior was down, but he didn't know how many remained. Still, one rifle less changed the odds. He looked around, orienting himself and searching for threats. The land was quiet, his murder unobserved.

From the pond, he thought he saw a faint luminescence, a blue glow that emanated from the depths. The glow pulled at him, sparking a deep curiosity.

Elzeth felt it, too. "It's the nexus," he said, a surprising longing in his voice.

Tomas nodded. In time, they could investigate.

He supposed the blind could be his next stop. It was as good a place as any.

Tomas returned to hands and knees, crawling along the outside edge of the rise. The decision was an assumption, a guess there weren't that many guards here. A pair with rifles seemed reasonable. One to watch the approach from town and one to watch the nexus from the blind.

They were only guesses, though, so he moved slowly, relying on his hearing to detect other shooters.

The passing of time concerned him. The cover of night only lasted so long, but he supposed if he cleared the defenses in the night, the day could be spent exploring. Thanks to Gaven, Tomas didn't expect the defenders to receive reinforcements anytime soon. Still, he'd rather finish before the sun came up.

The blind didn't take him long to reach. As he neared, he caught a closer look for the first time. It appeared as though someone had dug a decent hole and covered it with a piece of worn leather. The leather was tented slightly, allowing rain to run off and a slight breeze to pass through. A single rifle barrel moved slightly, pointed in the direction of the nexus.

Tomas considered a few approaches, but he couldn't figure out a way to completely surprise the shooter within and still get a clean kill.

He gripped his knife and slid into the blind from the side opposite the rifle barrel.

The hole was deeper than he expected, but there was only one man within.

"Hells, Jak," the shooter said, never taking his eyes off the nexus. "You gave me quite the fright. I didn't hear you coming at all."

Tomas slid his knife into the man's back, covering his mouth as he did. The man died a few moments later, eyes wide.

Tomas let him down gently, propping him up against the edge of the hole. He brought the rifle in and quickly examined it. It and the other were two of the same type. Tomas tossed the weapon in the corner. Even holding it made his hands feel dirty.

Once his eyes adjusted to the darkness of the blind, Tomas looked for other clues.

The blind appeared to be the center of all activity around the nexus. It held several days' worth of supplies, including food and water. Even more interesting, it had four bedrolls stored within.

Tomas swore softly to himself. Two more church soldiers to find and kill before he could freely explore the nexus. He was already feeling the first hints of weariness from his efforts thus far.

But he supposed there was nothing for it. He climbed out of the blind the way he'd come in.

Only to see two warriors approaching the blind, their white uniforms reflected in the dual light of the moons.

Their eyes met Tomas' and they drew their swords.

They weren't snipers, but full-fledged knights.

19

Elzeth flared to life. Any weariness Tomas felt vanished, replaced by the energy to run leagues without stopping. He drew his own sword, and the battle was joined.

The knights spread out as they rushed him, revealing the amount of training the pair had probably completed together. The grass hissed as the wind suddenly picked up, obscuring the sound of the knights' footsteps.

Tomas dashed toward one, revealing his true strength. These two had to be the last left in the area, so there would be no one to whisper his secret to the knight commander. He closed the gap in two quick steps.

His speed surprised the knight, but the church didn't bestow knighthood on just anyone. Surprised or not, the knight parried Tomas' cut. Though a bit slow, it was fast enough to prevent any openings Tomas might exploit.

Their swords flickered in the moonlight, reflecting the pale red and whiteish blue of the planet's twin satellites. The knight cut, the swing starting low, slicing through the grass as though it wasn't even there.

Tomas danced back, impressed. Cutting through so much grass might seem easy to the untrained, but to do so with no loss of speed was evidence enough of the knight's skill.

The second knight joined the fight, attacking Tomas from another angle. Tomas tapped the man's stab off its line, then slid under a cut from the first knight.

Elzeth kept Tomas alive. A sharp exhale of breath marked the beginning of a cut. The whisper of a blade through grass let him know where his enemy's steel was. For two heartbeats there was no sound except that of feet twisting and shuffling in the grass and the soft song of sharpened blades slicing the wind. Then swords would meet, the sound of steel on steel jarringly loud.

It was an elegant, if deadly, dance. Here there was none of the fierce brutality of untrained warriors.

But it was the elegance of the fight that doomed the knights.

Knights were among the best trained swords in the known world. For all his hate of the church, even Tomas admitted that. But their training was classical, and assumed their opponents would be either untrained, or schooled in another classical form. The knights were young, and their techniques hadn't been sharpened by the endless years of war Tomas had fought.

Tomas cut low, his sword aimed at ankles and calves. The first knight he attacked retreated, unsure how to respond to such low attacks. Tomas pressed his advance. The knight had no choice. He blocked low, but he wasn't trained to execute such blocks well. No classical technique cut so low.

Without Elzeth, such a technique would be fatal, leaving too many openings for counterattack.

The poor defense left the knight off balance for a moment, and that was all Tomas needed.

The knight fell, clutching at the spurting wound.

The second knight maintained his composure. Of the two, he possessed more skill, and the loss of his partner didn't appear to affect him in any noticeable way. They passed and passed again. Tomas cut the knight, but not more than a scratch.

The knight pressed, his attacks relentless. But he wasn't fast enough to penetrate Tomas' defense. And he tired first. His cuts became a bit slower, and then it was over. Tomas got inside the knight's guard and finished the fight with one decisive cut.

The night fell silent. Their battle had taken them up to the top of the rise, and Tomas could see for miles.

It also made him visible to anyone near, but Tomas didn't worry. He breathed deeply as Elzeth returned to his waking slumber.

Off in the distance, a pair of shapes moved. They didn't resemble any creature Tomas could easily identify, and he assumed they were sagani. The creatures moved without haste, but they seemed to be approaching the nexus. Tomas observed them for a few moments more, then turned to look at the still pond below. "Do you sense anything?" he asked.

Elzeth was silent for several seconds. "An attraction, perhaps. It calls to me, but softly, as though through a thick wall."

"Shall we?"

"We didn't come all the way out here for the company."

Tomas walked down the rise, wary for others who might still be near. Although he assumed the four he'd killed were the extent of the church's defenses, he didn't accept his assumption as fact. That was a quick way to an early grave.

"I didn't recognize the two knights," Elzeth said.

Tomas thought back to the fight against the church in the street, recalling the eight faces the Family had struggled against.

Elzeth was right.

"The church had ten knights here," Tomas said.

"Now five. They won't be happy about that."

"Can't please everyone."

Tomas reached the edge of the pond. As he'd seen from a distance, the pond appeared deep, with walls of stone. He looked around, trying to judge just how far from the top of the rise they'd descended. He supposed they were a bit lower than the land surrounding the rise.

The soft blue glow came from one side of the pond, almost like a glowing window underwater.

"What is it about the nexus that is worth ten knights?" Tomas asked. "They didn't even send that many after us during the war."

"Only one way to find out," Elzeth answered. He didn't bother to hide the excitement in his voice.

Tomas understood. This was the closest they'd come to a nexus in all of their wanderings. Hells, there had been plenty of times when Tomas had been convinced the whole idea of a nexus was preposterous. This was their first solid evidence.

Tomas looked around the crater again, but as before, there was nothing. For all he knew there were another half-dozen snipers out there, hiding in the grass. But he heard nothing, smelled nothing, and saw nothing.

He stripped off his clothes until he was naked, then grabbed a knife. It wasn't much, but he couldn't stomach the idea of being completely unarmed.

He dipped his toes in the water, then grunted. It was warm.

He took a few deep breaths and dove in.

The water wasn't just warm, it was unnaturally clean. As he dove deeper, he saw dust float from his arms and drop deeper into the pond. Everything about the pond unnerved him, but he forced those uncertainties away.

Down he went, the pressure building. He couldn't have been more than ten or fifteen feet down, but somehow it felt much deeper.

Then he was before the hole in the rock, the glow emanating from within. He swam forward, the hole just wide enough for him to slip through. He entered slowly, avoiding the sharp edges of the hole.

On the other side was an underwater cavern.

He blinked as his eyes adjusted to the brightness within.

The nexus was a glowing stone, appearing to be some sort of uncut diamond, perhaps. Though Tomas couldn't say why, he couldn't view it as mere rock. Not because it was glowing, but because it was beating.

He couldn't say how he knew. The light of the nexus remained steady, and it gave no outward appearance, but all the same, he was certain it beat in rhythm with his own heart.

This close, something inside of him responded to the call of the nexus. He felt himself drawn to it, and he swam closer. His lungs were starting to burn. He only had a few moments before he needed to turn around and swim back out, but it was so close, and he had to know more.

He reached out to touch it.

20

Touching the living stone was a mistake.

The moment his fingers came into contact with the glowing rock, a crashing wave of energy enveloped him. It was as if Elzeth had awoken, but had brought dozens of friends, too. Every muscle in Tomas' body clenched, and he almost let out what little air he had remaining to him.

Elzeth roared.

Tomas felt the sagani gather around his navel, pressing against all sides of him like Tomas' body had suddenly become a cage he needed to escape from.

Some of Tomas' precious air escaped as he fought the myriad threats to his focus.

He pulled his hand away, but it refused to move. Though he was connected only by the tips of his fingers, it was as if someone had come and nailed them in place. He pulled again, to no avail.

He almost planted his feet against the stone, then thought better of it. If they stuck, he'd have no hope at all.

"Elzeth!"

Power flowed like rapids through his arm. Elzeth gave no indication he'd heard Tomas. He continued to fight against Tomas' body.

Tomas' heart pounded. He desperately needed air. He wanted nothing more than to inhale, but it would be the last breath he ever took. Darkness swam at the edges of his vision, dimming even the light of the stone.

"Elzeth!"

This time he felt a flicker of peace, but the moment was lost in the roaring maelstrom of energy. Tomas forced himself to relax. No strength he possessed was enough.

But there was strength in surrender.

He'd learned that lesson as a younger man, and he applied it now.

The energy still flowed through him, but now it met less resistance. His arm still burned and quivered, but the pain was manageable.

"Elzeth." Tomas' call was clear and calm.

This time, Elzeth stilled himself.

"I need you."

There was movement within him. When Elzeth answered, his voice was drained of its normal vigor. "I don't want to let go."

"It will kill us both."

"There are worse fates."

In all their years together, Tomas had never known Elzeth to give up. "I don't want to die. Not yet."

He sensed the indecision in the sagani.

Then the flow of energy stopped. He still felt full to bursting, but it no longer traveled between him and the stone.

Elzeth became more still than Tomas had ever felt him, leaving Tomas dead and hollow inside.

As though he was alone.

He pulled, and his fingers drifted away from the stone without problem.

Tomas swam madly toward the opening. He scraped his arms, torso, and leg against the sharp rock as he passed through. Then he rose as fast as he could, the pale light of morning above him, blood from his cuts sinking deeper.

His head broke through the surface of the water and he gasped for air. Water filled his mouth and he coughed, but after a few moments of hacking and spitting, he was floating calmly in the pool.

Thankfully, no one was near. He floated on his back, looking up at the sky, thinking of nothing in particular. He could barely feel Elzeth at all. The sagani felt like a flickering flame after being doused with water. Elzeth was still there, still a part of him, but was just clinging to existence.

He hadn't come that close to death since the war.

Eventually, it was time to move. He swam to shore where he'd left his clothes. As he pulled himself out of the pond, he looked down to see how bad the cuts he'd gotten from the rocks were. He only found one on his side, where he remembered feeling a deep gash. Now it was barely more than a scratch. And as he watched, it faded to nothing.

Elzeth could heal him, but not like this. And besides, the sagani was still deathly quiet within.

Tomas twisted and craned his neck, looking for any other injuries, but he found nothing. Even a nagging pain in his back had vanished. He felt better than ever.

And that frightened him more than his brush with death.

"What was that?"

Elzeth stirred but didn't reply.

Tomas turned to his clothes. They were caked with

layers of dust, accumulated over miles of walking. Blood spatters dried on top of the dust. In short, they were filthy.

Elzeth felt like a jumbled mess, and Tomas had no chance of sneaking back into town without the cover of night. So he took his garments and washed them in the pool.

When he first washed his clothes, they created a small cloud of dust in the water, but within minutes the pond was clear as glass once again.

Everything about this place made his skin crawl.

He returned to the blind where he'd ambushed the second marksman and helped himself to supplies. The food wasn't great, but he'd survived on far worse.

Then he found a place where he could sit in the grass, watch the nexus, and think. The nexuses were incredibly powerful. Tomas couldn't say much more than that with any confidence, but he understood at least part of why the church found them so important. He lifted his clothes and checked his skin again. He was certain he'd been cut in several places. It was indisputable.

And yet he was healed and more. Through no effort of Elzeth.

What else could the nexuses do?

And how far would the church go to possess this one? It wasn't a large organization, although it proselytized constantly and grew daily. People were more difficult for the church to acquire than money, as far as he knew. Ten knights had to be nearly the full extent of the church's forces out here.

The Family wasn't much less terrifying. Though they didn't have the knights, they had plenty of skilled warriors they could call on. If the knight commander spoke true, they'd already begun.

So what could he do?

He chewed on the problem as he snacked on the food from the blind.

He had no brilliant solutions. Nothing solved the problem of two powerful entities dueling one another.

"You still alive?" he asked.

Elzeth grumbled. Even that reassured Tomas, though.

"What happened down there?"

Elzeth sighed. "I'm not sure."

Tomas waited for him to say more.

It took the sagani a while to find the words. "When you touched the stone, I felt connected to a power much deeper than anything I'd ever experienced. It was immense, and it was alive. And somehow, it and I were connected. I felt whole."

"You hadn't before?" Tomas interrupted.

"It was like the stone filled a part of me I didn't even know was empty," Elzeth said. "All I wanted was to remain connected to it. A part of me knew that if you died, then I would be free, and I would be a part of it forever, a part of something bigger. A part of something that truly under-stood what I was."

The longing in his voice clawed at Tomas' feelings. Nine days out of ten, Elzeth seemed content enough with their arrangement. On rare days, he even seemed grateful. But over the years Tomas had noticed there were more days where Elzeth was grouchier than usual. Days where it seemed he wanted to be elsewhere. They didn't speak much those days. Though Tomas didn't keep too close of track, those days seemed more frequent now than they once had.

Tomas hated the idea that Elzeth might feel trapped, true as it might be. "You wanted me to die, didn't you?"

A long pause.

"I did."

The admission wasn't surprising, but it cut deep. He'd never settled on a definition for his relationship with Elzeth. Friends didn't seem a strong enough word. But their choice to come together had been an act of desperation, and until today, they'd always assumed they were trapped together forever. They'd believed that when one died, they both died. And in most cases, that might still be true. No sagani they knew had ever survived the death of the host.

Elzeth knew him better than any human could.

Many had wished Tomas dead over the years, and he rarely took it personally.

Having Elzeth wish him dead felt like having his own sword masters wishing the same. "Why'd you let go of the connection, then?"

Elzeth didn't answer for a long time. When he did, his answer was far from satisfying. "Couldn't say."

Tomas swallowed the lump in his throat. "Thank you."

Elzeth went silent again, and Tomas understood he didn't want to talk much more.

Which was fine.

He still had to figure out how to keep this power out of the hands of both the Family and the church.

In time, he gave up searching for a solution. If one existed, he wasn't sure what it was.

He gathered up any useful supplies, then took the two rifles and threw them in the pond. He enjoyed watching the weapons sink down and out of sight.

Tomas left the nexus and began the journey back toward town. Around noon he stopped, found a secluded place in the grass, then lay down and went to sleep. Despite Elzeth's silence, he trusted the sagani would wake him if any danger approached.

When he woke, the sun was setting and the sky darkening. He stretched and ran through some of his forms while he waited for the full cover of night, then made for the town before Tolkin could rise.

He reached the town before long. Pairs of soldiers were stationed every thirty to forty feet in a loose cordon of the town, and more pairs of soldiers with dogs walked the perimeter, sniffing out any attempts at entrance or escape.

He hid in the grass and observed. Crawling through a gap between the guards wouldn't be particularly difficult. But it would be slow work, and the dogs gave him pause. If one came near while he was crawling, it would likely notice him.

So he watched, wondering if there was an order to their routes.

He quickly found there was not. The guards with the dogs wandered freely, making their movements almost impossible to predict.

He waited until a pair of guards with dogs had passed. He saw no others near, so he began his entrance back into town.

Gaven's soldiers impressed him more with every interaction. Guard duty was among the most difficult of duties to complete well, simply because it was usually so monotonous. These soldiers kept their discipline, seeking out dangers both from town and from the wild. The soldiers of the 34th didn't speak often, and when they did, it was in a whisper.

Even a stray sound would give him away.

Before long, Tomas' arms and shoulders began to burn. The energy he'd felt earlier in the day was gone.

Fortunately, no dogs came around in the time it took

him to pass the line. Alert as the sentries were, they didn't notice him as he slid like a snake through the grass.

Eventually he reached the edge of town, where he was able to stand and shake out his arms. He made his way back to Franz's inn, excited to spend the rest of the night asleep.

Franz was still awake when Tomas opened the front door, and he asked if Tomas needed any food. Despite his exhaustion, Tomas considered the offer. But he shook his head, climbed the stairs, and collapsed into his bed.

He woke the next morning to the sounds of a commotion down in the streets. Not conflict, as he'd heard several days ago, but a bustling activity. He went to the window and looked out just in time to see a column of soldiers marching out of town.

His stomach sank, and he heard the sound of slow, solid footsteps coming up the stairs. There was a firm knock on the door. "Come in," he said.

A soldier stepped inside and gave Tomas a short bow. Tomas guessed the message before the soldier spoke, and his guess was confirmed a few moments later. "The general would like to see you. We've been forced to leave earlier than we expected."

21

T omas took a few minutes to make sure he looked presentable, then made his way down the hall to the general's room. The messenger knocked and admitted him.

Gaven gave him a small nod of acknowledgement as he entered. The general was pouring over lists and figures, untangling the logistics that arose anytime hundreds of soldiers needed to move from one place to another. After a few minutes he shuffled the papers away and gave Tomas his full attention. "We're leaving today."

"A bit sooner than you expected."

Gaven nodded. "We got word of a series of brutal murders in a nearby town. Don't know much else, but we couldn't have stayed here much longer anyway. Both the church and the Family are behaving themselves, and we need to return to Tansai. My soldiers have been away from their families for too long."

"It's been nice having you here. Quiet. Don't suppose there's any way I could convince you to stay for another day or two?"

The general shook his head. "If it matters, I believe you. I haven't seen so many knights in one place since the war, and while the Family is doing the best they can to disguise their strength, it's a pretty futile attempt. And hells, I'd love to go toe-to-toe with them here, but without evidence, I can't risk it. It would be my head on a pike if I couldn't defend my actions. The government wants peace, but they're fools to think the way forward is free of confrontation. Both those forces are getting too strong for their own good."

Tomas had suspected the answer, but had to ask. He bowed to Gaven. "I appreciate your efforts, regardless, general. You've kept the fight in check for several days, and that's something."

"What will you do?" Gaven asked.

"I'm not sure," Tomas said, "but neither the Family nor the church seems to appreciate my visit, so perhaps it might be time for me to leave as well."

"You could join us," Gaven offered. "We're all on the same side now, and you seem like a man with some skill and honor. We could always use more like you."

Tomas bowed. "I appreciate the offer, general, truly. But I swore long ago I'd never take an order again."

Gaven took no offense. "May we all live long enough to make the same promise." Then his smile and good humor faded. "But be careful. No matter how strong you are, being alone is a weakness."

Tomas bowed. "Excellent advice. I will do my best to heed it. Safe travels, general."

Gaven matched the bow. "And to you, Tomas."

Tomas left and went down to the dining hall, where several of the officers were eating their last meal. They all wished him well, and Tomas returned their wishes as he ate his breakfast. But even Franz's excellent food couldn't free him from the worries that ran in circles through his thoughts.

Multiple murders in a nearby town? Probably the assassin the knight commander warned him about. It was too much of a coincidence to be anything else. Which meant the Family were the ones pulling the army away. And that meant Jons believed he had the upper hand.

And if Jons believed he had the upper hand, he probably did.

The assassin must be something else to inspire such confidence.

"Another host?" Elzeth asked.

Tomas startled at the interruption. He'd been so distracted he hadn't even felt the sagani stir. And Elzeth had been almost entirely silent since the nexus. "If it's one person, it almost has to be," Tomas said. "I can't imagine Jons' confidence would be so high otherwise."

He picked at his food, not hungry but knowing he needed to eat. His theory was all guesses and intuition, but it felt right. The story made sense, and no others did. Tomas leaned back in his chair. "Hells."

"Maybe I should have just killed you back at the nexus," Elzeth said. "Saved us both a few days."

It was a joke, an attempt at reconciliation. Which Tomas appreciated. But it held a bitter edge, a sharp truth. Elzeth wanted the nexus, and a part of him, at least, regretted his decision to let Tomas live. Even after a day to think about it.

"Do you really care what happens to the nexus?" Elzeth asked. "It's one of dozens, if not hundreds. And at best you can delay them. But we both know you won't stay here and protect it forever. You're risking everything and gaining nothing."

"If I leave, Franz and his family will die."

"And you've given them every opportunity. They've made their choice. You can't be responsible for them, too."

Tomas watched Franz, scurrying around the dining hall, bowing deeply to the few remaining officers as they paid for the last of their lodgings. He never stopped for more than a few seconds. He was always either serving, cleaning, or conversing. On his face was a constant smile, unaffected, a soft radiance following him wherever he walked.

Tomas cursed again.

He hated to agree with Elzeth. But the sagani was right. Even under the best possible outcome, he only saved the town for a while.

"You're not going to have many more opportunities to leave," Elzeth observed. "No one will make their move for a day or two, just to make sure the army is clear, but then it's over. And you know that the second the cordon is lifted the knight commander is going to send others to check on the nexus."

Tomas finished the cold food left on his plate. "I'd like to stay."

He wondered if he and Elzeth would truly disagree. Over the years they had argued plenty. Almost by habit they took opposite sides of most debates. But Tomas had come to view the arguments more as a ceremony than a fight. Elzeth kept him from jumping into foolish situations, or at the very least, made sure he jumped into them fully aware of his foolishness.

Eventually, though, they had always come to an agreement. At first, Tomas had attributed their compatibility to coincidence. He'd simply become host to a sagani who shared his temperament and beliefs. Now he wasn't so sure. He suspected that as Elzeth had gained consciousness, that development was influenced by Tomas. They weren't the same, nor were they two halves of a whole. They remained separate entities in one body. But it was impossible to spend every day with the same person and not be influenced by them.

This felt different. The events at the nexus bothered Elzeth. Tomas knew no other explanation for the long silences. He got the sense that if Elzeth couldn't join the nexus, the sagani wanted as much distance between him and it as possible. He wanted to forget it, seeking distance the same way an alcoholic sought peace in the bottom of his cup.

Tomas looked again at Franz, cleaning up the last of the tables. He liked the old man, but he knew, if he had to choose, who would have his vote, no matter how dishonorable it felt. "I won't do this without you," he said.

Elzeth still didn't respond, torn between his competing desires.

Eventually, he acquiesced. "Fine."

"Thank you."

Tomas stood up, the last customer in the dining hall. Franz bowed as he left. He climbed the stairs to his room and watched out the window as the remaining soldiers gathered and left.

As with everything the 34th did, their exit was quick and orderly. Tomas bet that by noon the town would be empty once again.

And then the final battle would begin.

22

Tomas was right.

By noon, it was as if the army had never existed at all. He watched as much of the street as his window would allow, and it was deserted for as far as the eye could see.

The difference struck him with the same strength as it had when he'd first visited the town. Over the past several days he'd become used to the sight of others walking the street in daylight. Shops had been open, and even the few remaining neutral residents had milled about. The town had almost seemed normal.

No more.

The wind blew down barren streets, kicking up dust on its way out of town. Everyone knew what the departure of the army meant. A few families had left in the army's trail, knowing they had little to gain by staying. Those that stayed remained indoors, and probably away from windows. Glass did little to stop a bullet.

Tomas felt the impending battle as a heaviness in his chest. Powerful as the nexus was, it seemed a poor excuse for all the death the town had already seen. And there was more yet to come. He rested for a while, only coming awake for a few moments when he heard a note being slid underneath his door.

Elzeth woke him in the late afternoon. He stretched and ran through his forms, paying particular attention to how his body felt. He found no flaws in the healing he'd experienced back at the nexus. His muscles responded with a vigor he hadn't felt for many years. And it still frightened him. He felt a little as though someone had wound a clock backward on him and placed him in a younger body.

The note was written in Elissa's sharp hand. It stated that Boss Jons expected him in the gambling hall at nightfall.

Tomas thought he would have at least another day. But it made no real difference. He went downstairs. Perhaps this would finally be the time Franz and his family listened to him.

Inaya served him, Franz apparently too consumed with his tasks in the kitchen to play host as well. When she set his first course before him, he asked, "Is there any chance your family will consider leaving?"

She shook her head, then glanced back to the kitchen. She leaned in closer. "I've thought about it, but there's no way for me to leave on my own." She sat in the chair across from him. "Mara worries me most of all. Eiro might have been a horrible man, but he was her son, and she loved him. Boss Jons, he would just make us pay extra tribute for the rest of our lives. But Mara, she'll find a way to avenge her son, especially me."

Tomas gritted his teeth. "Then why won't they leave?"

Inaya's smile stilled his frustration. "You haven't had a home in a long time, have you?"

He looked at her, confused.

"They built this place with their own hands, and that was after enduring the journey to come out here, well before there were any real roads. This is a place that is special to them. It's worth fighting for, and I think for them, even worth dying for."

"But they could just leave! Inns can be built anywhere, a life made in better lands."

"True, but that isn't how they see it." She focused more on him. "Why haven't you left?"

"That's a question I've been asking myself all day."

"And?"

"Your grandfather's food is too good to leave behind."

She rolled her eyes. "You'll get yourself killed."

"I'd rather not."

"Word is that Jons called in one of the Family's best assassins. Not even hosts are safe."

The last of Tomas' good humor died at the mention of hosts. "Your grandda shouldn't have said anything. It puts you in danger."

"Grandma had already guessed, and I was there when he confirmed it," Inaya said. "It's not like it puts us in any more danger."

"You don't want to cross paths with a church inquisitor."

She didn't have a response to that, but Tomas could see she wasn't as afraid as she should have been. Out here, the arm of the church responsible for inquisitions was probably little more than a story told to frighten misbehaving children. And legally, inquisitors didn't exist.

But that didn't make them any less real, or any less terrifying.

Tomas had only ever crossed paths with one, but that was one too many.

Inaya bit on her lower lip, then squared her shoulders. Tomas knew her question before she even spoke it. Part of the reason he'd come west was so he'd never have to answer it again.

"What's it like?"

Tomas looked at her. He should tell her to leave. Anything she learned would only endanger her further. If she'd asked three days ago, he might have.

But after encountering the nexus, his secrecy seemed a mistake. Humans didn't know enough about the sagani, and if the church had their way, most humans never would. He hated the risk sharing entailed, but maybe the way to fight the church wasn't with the sword, but with the tale of his experiences. "It's like sharing my head with someone else."

"It can read your thoughts?"

"Not exactly. More like he can sense them. He knows when I'm angry, and he's always with me. When you're that close, it's hard to hide."

"He's—always with you?"

Tomas nodded.

"Even—?" She had the decency not to ask the rest.

Tomas nodded again. "Just one of the many reasons I'm not married. Hard to make it work with three."

Franz called from the kitchen, and Inaya ran, grabbed the food, and came back. "How did you become a host?"

"The short version is that he tried to kill me when I was exploring some mountains. Came close to succeeding. We were both near death when suddenly, I felt a connection to him." He looked down at the table. "It's hard to describe the next part. I went through a lot, and it hurt unlike anything I've ever experienced before or since. But when I came to, there was just—us."

Memories arose unbidden. The clear, powdery snow of

the high elevations. The trampled area around him. Blood, turned brown by its exposure to air. Too much blood to survive losing. And the knowledge that he was no longer alone. He'd held onto his life that day, but he'd lost something else.

Inaya seemed to read into his thoughts. "Do you regret it?"

"Sometimes."

"What did you find at the nexus?"

Tomas shook his head. "Did Franz tell you everything?"

"We're not much on secrets in this home."

"The knowledge will only get you in more trouble."

She ignored him, waiting for him to answer.

He sighed. "A power, stronger and stranger than anything I've encountered. When I touched it, it healed my wounds. And I have the sense that was only the beginning of what its capable of."

She stood up from the table. "Thank you for telling me."

He nodded.

She took a step, then hesitated. "And Tomas?"

"Hmm?"

"I'm glad you're here to help us. I'm glad you aren't running." She bowed to him, then hurried away. Tomas saw her face had flushed red.

He finished his meal in silence, lost in the memories of his past, worried about the near future.

Then he stood and left for the hall.

It was time to see what Jons wanted him for.

23

When Tomas entered the hall, it almost looked as if the fight had started without him. Or, at the very least, that the fight was about to start without him. Near the bar sat a large group of men and women, most of them with several drinks before them. They focused on finding the bottom of their cups as quickly as possible.

Across the hall, sitting on chairs borrowed from the card tables, were the remaining Family. They twitched and shuffled with the nervous energy that came before a battle.

If the battle was between these two factions, the Family was outnumbered maybe two to one. But judging from the difficulty some of the mercenaries were having sitting upright, the difference in numbers might not mean much.

Tomas' attention, though, was drawn to a small man sitting off by himself, his chair tilted back on two legs as he leaned against a wall. The man's eyes drooped, but Tomas saw a sharp gaze underneath. His sword rested against the wall, too.

Tomas didn't recognize the man, but it was his aloofness

that identified him as the assassin the knight commander had warned him about.

The assassin's gaze only flickered over Tomas briefly, then continued roving around the room.

The Family stared daggers at the backs of the mercenaries, who were doing an admirable job of ignoring the glares. Though a clear and wide path existed between the factions, Tomas didn't advance for fear of getting caught in between.

Neither Jons nor Mara were present.

Tomas stepped to the side so that he wasn't in the path of the door. Then he, too, grabbed a chair and leaned it against a wall. Nothing to do but wait and see how the situation developed.

Jons appeared at the balcony above the main hall about ten minutes later. He saw Tomas, but gave him no acknowledgment.

Tomas smiled to himself. It was a bad sign when your enemies didn't even pretend to show proper etiquette.

The boss' appearance froze the room. None of the mercenaries picked up their cups while he watched, and the Family looked like they were one word away from drawing their swords and slaughtering the mercenaries.

But unless that assassin was truly special, the loss of the mercenaries would amount to the end of the Family's involvement in this town.

Jons opened his mouth, but didn't speak. He looked over the room once again, then came down the stairs until he was standing in the middle of everything. When he spoke, it was quietly. "It's time."

For several seconds, no one moved.

Then one of the men spoke at the bar. His words were clear, if low. He was one of the few who hadn't gotten lost in drink. "We're not going."

The Family tensed even further, hands grasping at hilts. Jons held out a hand to stop them. "What did you say?"

The mercenary at the bar took a long breath and spun around slowly on his stool. He might have had a beer or two in him, but his voice and gaze remained steady. "We're not going," he repeated.

"You're acting as though you have a choice," Jons said.

"Of course we have a choice. Anyone can see that if you kill us you lose any chance at winning this fight. But if we attack tonight, we lose the fight anyway. We're less than half the strength we were, and now they have no reason to hide the rifles. As soon as we march down there, they'll open fire. Those of us lucky enough to survive will face the knights." The mercenary shook his head. "Your money's good, but it's no good if we're dead."

Say one thing for mercenaries, they weren't fools. Tomas detested those willing to kill for coin, but they were dependable in their own way. You could always depend on them to do what earned them the most, and gave them the best chance to spend said money.

Jons' gaze lingered on the mercenary spokesman, then swept over the rest of the group. He pursed his lips. "And what would you suggest? If I were to let you leave, my cause would be equally lost. Do you seek more money?"

The mercenary again shook his head. "All the money in the world doesn't matter to a dead man." He paused. "No, you're paying us fair, there's no arguing that. But walking down that street tonight is suicide. We've been talking, and we think it's best if you hire on some more swords. Once you've got your numbers back up, we'll fight for you."

"You'd remain here while I recruited?" The corner of Jons' mouth turned up in a smile.

The mercenary noticed the smile, and although it seemed to unsettle him, he stood his ground. "Of course."

"And it goes without saying that you'd continue to enjoy my hospitality and earn coin while I did so."

"Seems only fair, given all the chores you've been having us do."

A grin broke out on Jons' face.

Elzeth swore.

Tomas agreed. Jons' smile twisted his stomach.

Jons turned to the assassin against the opposite wall. "Aron, would you come here, please?"

Aron nodded and stood up, every move slow and deliberate. He walked with an uneven gait, almost seeming lazy. His steps were slow and unhurried.

And he left his sword up against the wall.

Tomas tensed, then forced himself to relax. Aron's demeanor didn't fool him for a moment, but he'd rather not reveal that.

It worked on the mercenary, though. As Aron came to stand next to Jons, the mercenary visibly relaxed.

After all, the man had left his sword behind.

"This is Aron," Jons said. "Have you met Aron?"

The mercenary shook his head. He looked confused, as though some part of his mind was warning him just how much danger he was in, but he couldn't spot it.

"Aron is the one who will help us kill the knights. He's the one who will stop the rifles. You'll have nothing to worry about."

"He doesn't look like much."

Tomas had to agree with the mercenary there. The man was short, probably not much over five feet tall. His hair was unkempt, and he looked skinny enough to break like a twig.

Jons smirked. "I assure you, he's up to the task. Prepare for battle."

The mercenary's eyes turned hard.

"No."

Jons gestured and Aron's arm blurred.

Elzeth swore again. Tomas clenched his muscles as the sagani roared within.

The cut had been almost too fast for Tomas to follow. Had he been standing in the mercenary's place, he didn't think even he would have been able to react in time.

Just as quick, Aron's hand was down by his side again.

The mercenary's eyes widened, then rolled back in his head. A thin blade jutted from his neck.

Tomas wasn't sure the rest of the hall even realized what had happened yet.

Then the mercenary fell and the uproar ensued. Mercenaries were shouting as the Family drew their weapons. Jons and Aron stood in the middle of the storm, no one daring to come close.

Jons allowed the chaos for a few moments more, then raised his hand. The mercenaries, constantly glancing back at Aron, quieted. Aron sauntered back to his seat and returned to the exact position he'd been in when Tomas had entered.

"We're attacking the knights. Aron will clear the watchtower, and between him and Tomas, we'll have nothing to fear. You'll live to enjoy your coin," Jons said. "And if you argue with any of my orders, well, Aron will give everyone another demonstration. Am I understood?"

The mercenaries nodded.

"I can't hear you. Am I understood?"

A chorus of yeses came from the group.

"Good. Now prepare. We'll leave in a few minutes."

Jons climbed back up the stairs and disappeared. The mercenaries gave each other looks, but they obeyed. Weapons were checked and drinks finished.

Tomas ignored the activity. His eyes were on Aron.

That strike had been faster than anything Tomas could duplicate. Which meant Aron was a host, too.

And quite possibly the stronger warrior.

24

A ron left the hall first, obeying Jons' command. Tomas watched the assassin vanish into the shadows of the building, disappearing like a ghost. Aron traveled in the direction of the church watchtower.

Jons didn't wait to be assured of Aron's success. He turned his attention back to the assortment of warriors remaining in the hall. They had formed up in what could loosely be considered a column, with the mercenaries in front and the Family behind.

Jons looked them over one last time, and when no one spoke out against him, led them from the hall, a smaller and quieter repeat of the battle several days ago. Tomas felt little of the nervous excitement they'd possessed on that first battle. He walked among the mercenaries, who behaved as though their deaths were all but certain.

He wasn't sure they were wrong.

The knights emerged from the mission as soon as Jons and his warriors were all in the street. They stood tall on their end of town, waiting for their enemies. All five of the remaining knights were present.

Tomas breathed deeply as Elzeth's energy built within. The body's natural instinct when encountering such strength was to tense, but the energy needed to flow. It was just one of many lessons they'd had to teach themselves over the years. Tomas shook out his arms and rolled his neck in a large circle, jumping a few times to stay loose.

They passed Franz's inn, and a few steps later they were in church territory. Not only that, but they were well in range of the rifles of the watchtower. Tomas glanced up at the silent structure. The dead mercenary had the right of it. Now that the rifles weren't a surprise, there was no point in the church not using them.

But the tower remained dark and still.

Apparently, Jon's faith in Aron's skill hadn't been misplaced.

After the display Tomas had seen, he wasn't surprised either.

The knight commander glanced up at the tower, then squinted. His posture stiffened and his hand went straight to his sword. He barked a low command and the other knights joined him. As one, they unsheathed their weapons.

In most circumstances, five blades against the advancing horde would have seemed like a suicidal stand. But the difference in skill between the mercenaries and the knights more than made up for the knights' lack of numbers.

But now Jons had Aron and Tomas.

The knights had no chance.

Tomas saw the tip of the knight commander's blade wobble, just for a moment. He was no fool. He didn't know exactly what was coming for him, but he knew well enough what this advance meant.

Aron emerged from the shadows of an alley and joined them, taking up position not far from Tomas. Both hosts were among the mercenaries, and the stench of drink was heavy in the air.

Jons had ordered the mercenaries to take the lead back in the hall. At first, when Tomas watched the Family line up behind the sellswords, he'd thought it was just to keep the hired help in line.

But he didn't think that was it, anymore. Yes, the arrangement prevented the mercenaries from running, but it made the mercenaries the bodies that would clog up the fight and slow down the knights. And had Aron failed, the mercenaries would have been the first to give their lives to reveal as much.

Not only that, but every dead mercenary was one more contract Jons didn't have to honor.

None of it was particularly surprising, but Tomas suppressed a shudder as he thought of Jons at his back.

If Tomas had to choose the lesser of two evils, the Family still beat the church, but Jons made the race close.

He discarded the thoughts and brought his focus to the battle at hand. The knights were trouble enough, and he suspected Aron had an eye on him as well.

"At least you won't be bored," Elzeth said.

The advance was fairly orderly until the group of mercenaries near the front decided that they had had enough. With fierce yells, they charged forward.

It was all the encouragement others needed. Soon, every mercenary was charging the knights.

The knights met the charge with a sturdy defense and quick deaths. The mercenaries fell as though they were nothing but blades of grass before the steel of the knights. But by the time the mercenaries realized the extent of their mistake, it was too late. The knights were among them and there was no escape. The Family behind them wouldn't allow them to give ground.

Tomas stepped over the soon-to-be-corpses and met a pair of knights. Six feet to his right, Aron engaged another pair.

Tomas' opponents held their swords as though they'd been born with them in hand. They danced over corpses, flicked deadly attacks aside with casual grace, and gave ground whenever it was required.

Tomas' advance was steady, but they denied him victory. Neither opponent was flawless, but the way the two knights moved as one, they were good enough to stay alive.

Aron brought down the knight commander's partner, the young woman Tomas had so enjoyed tormenting. Her death earned Aron the attention of the last knight, who had been fighting alone.

Jons shouted something Tomas didn't catch, and suddenly there were Family all around him, lending their strength and their steel to the execution of the knights. In their excitement, Tomas allowed himself to fall back, just a little. He wasn't comfortable with so many Family swords around and behind him.

With the brief freedom, Tomas studied Aron. The assassin's technique was straightforward and brutal, a system based on the shortest lines between him and his target. Straight, quick jabs and sharp kicks, all precisely aimed, seemed his primary skills.

And he was faster than Tomas. His hands were as quick as any Tomas had ever seen, and his aim unerringly true. Both his opponents were bleeding from multiple wounds, and it appeared that only the extraordinary skill of the knight commander kept them alive.

It couldn't last. Aron was just too fast.

And then what?

Tomas wasn't convinced he would win against Aron either.

He didn't have time to answer the question. The knights he'd faced were fighting back against the Family and gaining ground. Swords came for Tomas, and he joined the fray once again, noting that several Family had died while he watched Aron.

Good riddance.

Bodies pressed against him. Not enough to squeeze the breath from him, but enough to interfere with his swings. He took one cut from a knight, a shallow slice along his left arm.

Frustrated by one of the Family on his right, a larger man, Tomas shoved him at a knight.

The man swore and the knight sliced through his neck, but in that moment, Tomas stepped around and killed the knight. Both Family and knight fell together.

The last knight opposing Tomas fell easily, simply overwhelmed by the number of swords he had to fight off. Tomas struck the killing blow while the knight locked swords with another Family.

Tomas stepped away from the Family that had closed in on him. They'd been useful allies for a few minutes, but with the first fight over, he was already looking to the second.

To his right, Aron and the knight commander stood about six feet apart from one another. The knight commander was bleeding from at least three different wounds, but if he experienced any pain, he didn't show it. Aron, on the other hand, looked bored.

"He's got to be burning up," Elzeth said. "That speed is too much."

"Somehow I don't think he's going to listen to your concerns," Tomas said.

He took in the rest of the battlefield. The fighting had been quick, but the results were no less bloody. All the mercenaries were dead or dying, and Tomas only counted four or five Family besides Jons still standing. That number seemed too small, but he'd been distracted by the fight for a while.

Tomas considered the scene before him. He'd never have a better chance at attacking Aron than right now. With the knight commander's help, perhaps they would have a chance. Tomas leaned forward, ready to leap as soon as Aron's full attention was on the knight.

It was time to betray the Family for good.

He'd just finished the thought when the first bullet struck him.

25

T he bullet punched into his left shoulder, just below the collarbone. It tore out the back of his body, somehow managing to miss every bone on its short but brutal journey through him.

The impact spun him around and sent him toward the ground. As he fell a second bullet cracked the air above him, where he'd stood just a moment before.

Tomas hit the ground hard, his cry of pain cut short by his teeth slamming together. He landed facing Aron and the knight commander, who still dueled in the street. The knight commander was giving up ground fast, and Aron had a smirk on his face.

"Move!" Elzeth shouted.

The sagani's fire was white-hot. Much of Elzeth's power focused on his shoulder, knitting flesh and viscera together. But some went to Tomas' limbs, giving him the strength to push back the shock of the impact.

He pushed himself up with his left hand, the action sending blinding spikes of pain through his shoulder. Then he sheathed his sword and ran.

Two more bullets came hunting for his heart. One passed over his right shoulder while the other sliced through the outside of his right thigh. It drew a hot line of blood, but Tomas grimaced against the pain as he sprinted for cover.

Within a heartbeat he'd put a shop between him and the church watchtower.

He didn't settle for the first available cover. His wounds demanded time to heal, and time required distance. Sticking close to the buildings so his retreat wouldn't be seen from the watchtowers, he made his way a couple of houses down.

Curtains snapped shut in nearby windows. Tomas couldn't make out the figures behind them, but he had no doubt his movements were being followed by the few remaining citizens. But no one opened their door to lend him aid. He swore.

He didn't believe those that remained were staunch allies of one faction or the other. In his travels, he'd found that most were like Franz: decent people just doing the best they could to get by. But that didn't mean they would keep his movements secret. They owed him nothing, and if providing information to his pursuers kept them out of harm's way, he could hardly fault them. The same impulse would keep their doors shut to him.

He understood them, but understanding didn't cool his anger or his frustration at them. It would be almost impossible to hide while every eye was watching the streets.

One problem at a time.

He slumped against a house, closing his eyes and resting. Elzeth worked on the wounds. The graze on his thigh was already lightly scarred over, but the wound on his shoulder still burned. Tomas lifted up his shirt so he could look at it. Elzeth had already healed most of the viscera and was working his way outward. Tomas saw the skin slowly reform.

As Elzeth worked, Tomas' vision swam.

"Hells," Tomas said.

And then he was somewhere else, without thought. There was just experience, an openness to life as it unfolded before him. His sight was vivid, the world full of a rich and varied spectrum of colors. Smells wafted through the air. The scent of pine trees after a rain, fresh and green. The songs of the small birds nesting in those trees, warbling as they sang to potential mates.

Some shred of Tomas remained. He recognized this place. The ironwood forests.

And then even that scrap of thought vanished.

He ate when he was hungry and slept when he was tired. Otherwise, he roamed back and forth, with no particular purpose or destination. Until one day when he felt a pull.

He still roamed over wide swaths of mountainside, but now, every day when he slept he found himself farther north than the day before.

He wasn't alone. Others like him did the same. There was no competition, not among them. They acknowledged one another as they passed, but no more. Each of them headed north.

Others did, too. The mountains were becoming crowded. Mostly with the odd creatures who walked on two legs, who tramped loudly, and whose sharp weapons could kill with such ease. He didn't like those creatures. He avoided them when he could.

Then Tomas was back, no longer lost in Elzeth's memories. The houses of the town slowly steadied. The streets were quiet, but Tomas didn't feel like he'd been out of it for that long.

Aron had cleared the tower. That didn't seem up for dispute. No one had fired on Jons' assembly as they advanced. The knight commander had been surprised by the fact, and certainly hadn't had time to send more of his warriors to the tower.

"Which meant it was the Family who shot you," Elzeth finished the thought for him.

"Thought they'd at least have the decency to wait until the battle was over," Tomas said.

But he supposed it had been. Aron seemed more than competent enough to kill the knight commander. The Family had betrayed him before he could turn on Aron. If it hadn't resulted in the bullet through his shoulder, he might have been impressed.

He looked at his shoulder again. The flesh was still coming together, but it wouldn't be more than a minute or two before he could act again. The shoulder would take longer to fully heal, but it was good enough to fight with, at least for a while.

What to do?

The Family now had rifles and Aron. In one decisive move, they had become the undisputed rulers of town.

And he had helped them.

He swore at himself. He'd underestimated Jons.

Fighting Aron would have been difficult before. Now with protection from the rifles, it would be next to impossible.

Franz.

They'd be after the innkeeper and his family soon enough. But Jons would also expect him there.

Elzeth finished healing the wound and Tomas rotated

his shoulder. It ached, but considering he'd been shot only a few minutes ago, he couldn't complain.

He had to leave town. He hated the idea of abandoning Franz and his family, but the only way to keep fighting was to stay alive.

Tomas stood. The town remained quiet, pretending for the moment it was someplace more normal, a place where good folk went to bed at a decent time.

Anywhere else, the silence would have been comforting. Here, it made his heart race just a bit faster. The battle between the church and the Family was over.

Once again, he kept himself close to homes as he escaped. Thanks to Gaven's presence and the few days of peace it had brought, Tomas now understood the town's layout well. He slid from shadow to shadow, always out of sight of the church watchtower.

He'd only made it a few houses away when the sounds of uneven footsteps reached his ears. He pressed his back against the wall of the house he was using for cover, then slid lower.

The knight commander emerged from an alley about two houses away. He looked worse than Tomas felt. Blood soaked his white uniform from no fewer than half a dozen cuts. Another gash had been opened on his left leg, causing him to limp.

Had Tomas been a bit closer, he might have tried to kill the commander himself.

But it was clear the commander was running from someone.

Then the church soldier turned and started half-running, half-shuffling toward Tomas. Tomas swore under his breath, and a second later, the knight commander saw him.

Tomas sprung at the knight, his sword clearing its sheath in one quick cut.

How the knight spun out of the way defied belief. It wasn't the motion of a host. It wasn't fast enough for that. But the knight seemed to have a preternatural sense of where Tomas was going to strike.

The counter was slow. Tomas avoided it with ease, but before he could respond, a third person stepped into the street. Tomas saw Aron's hand come up and stepped back. A second later a throwing knife cut through the space between him and the knight.

"I didn't think you'd still be in town," Aron said to Tomas. "And I certainly didn't think you'd still be fighting against the knights." Aron shrugged. "I suppose it makes this easier, though."

The knight commander looked between Aron and Tomas. He spat, "Demons!" and ran off, his leg still giving him trouble.

Aron looked undecided, but only for a moment. Then he shrugged and turned to face Tomas. "Eh, he won't get very far. Let's kill you first."

26

A stiff breeze picked up, and Tomas thought he caught the scent of a summer storm off in the distance. Dust swirled around his ankles as he stood across from Aron. "Don't suppose it would do much good to point out you're letting the knight commander get away."

"Not much." Aron's smile was without warmth. "You pissed off the boss and his wife something fierce when you killed their kid, even if he was scum."

"There aren't many of us left."

Aron shrugged. "Can't say it's something I think about much. Never could find the time to worry about much besides myself, to tell the truth."

They circled each other warily. Then Aron took a step back, delaying the battle a moment longer. "There is one thing I've been curious about, though. Jons says you served in the war, but he also says he ain't seen none of the tics from you. Says it took him a while to figure out you were a host. How you been alive so long and not as mad as all get-out?"

"Is the secret worth my life?"

"Hells, no."

"Then I'm afraid I'm going to have to pass on sharing that tidbit."

Aron shrugged again, a behavior Tomas was finding more annoying with every occurrence. "Suit yourself, I suppose. But I ain't here to kill you."

Tomas frowned at that.

"Told ya. You pissed Boss Jons and Mara off. They don't just want you dead. I mean, they'd still pay me if you were, but they'll pay me more if you're alive. Boss Jons, he says he's got plans. And I'm sure if I ask nicely he'll get you to tell me how you're still alive and pretending you ain't one of us somehow. Probably something he wants to know anyway."

Tomas' stomach turned to ice. He didn't want to die, but he'd come to peace with that, at least. He'd rather not contemplate the other options.

"Some people just deserve to die," Elzeth said.

Tomas agreed. He attacked. His cut was clean, and while he felt his freshly knit flesh pull and stretch as he struck, it was a killing swing.

Aron wasn't there.

The other host had stepped back, then entered again into the space Tomas' sword had just cut through. He lashed out at Tomas, tracing a pale red arc as his sword reflected Tolkin's light.

Tomas let the blade pass in front of him, whispering death. They both twisted, each seeking that moment of advantage that would determine the victor. Swords clashed and broke apart, Tomas' strikes as quick as lightning.

Off in the distance he noticed a flicker of light. Several seconds later a low rumble of thunder muted the shuffling of the hosts' feet.

They traded another flurry of cuts. Tomas scored a thin cut against Aron's upper arm, but it had come at the cost of two on his chest.

Tomas couldn't think of any other warrior who moved so fast.

"He's got to be burning alive," Elzeth observed. "How long do you think he can continue?"

Tomas couldn't answer as he retreated before another flurry of Aron's cuts. Then they broke apart, each catching their breath.

"Long enough," he finally answered.

Tomas believed he was a little stronger, and he definitely felt more experienced. But he wasn't sure that was enough against Aron. The assassin's speed kept him safe, and he was smart enough not to extend himself too far. "I need more," Tomas said.

Elzeth didn't argue, despite the risks.

Aron was hopping from foot to foot, a smile plastered on his face. "It's been a few months since I've fought another host. And you're far better than he was. Hells, you're a better swordsman than me, even if it won't save you."

Tomas raised his sword.

Aron came forward so fast even Tomas could barely track him. If not for Elzeth's extra assistance, Tomas would have died just then. As it was, he still ended up stumbling away.

Aron's blade flickered, and again they met.

This time, Tomas didn't fare so well. Aron's movements were too fast for him to track, so he couldn't predict where the blows would come from. He couldn't get ahead of the assault.

He could defend himself, but just barely. Aron pushed

him back, further and further. Tomas' whole attention focused on the enemy in front of him.

If he could just get a moment to regain his composure, perhaps he'd have a chance, but Aron didn't give him a single second. The assassin pursued relentlessly, refusing to make a fatal mistake.

Something punched Tomas in the back, near his left hip.

Pain shot through his body as the report from the rifle reached his ears. The impact threw him off balance, and Aron used the moment to slice through his right forearm. Tomas' hand went limp and he dropped his sword.

Aron followed the cut with a kick straight to Tomas' chest.

The force of the kick stole what little balance Tomas had left. He fell onto his back, an impact that sent another spear of pain through him.

He swore.

Elzeth was working on his wounds, but Aron was prepared. He stepped forward and drove his sword through Tomas' shoulder, right where the bullet had passed earlier that evening. Tomas' vision swam, and for a second, blackness took him.

It couldn't have been long, because he woke up to his face being slapped from side to side.

In his peripheral vision he saw two of the Family appear, rifles trained on him. But he wasn't going anywhere. Aron had made sure of that.

Elzeth, never one predisposed to surrender, blazed hotter than ever.

The sagani's anger was matched by Tomas' own. To be shot in the back during a duel!

Aron shook his head, as though he understood Tomas' thoughts. "Winning is all that matters. Your antiquated notions of honor are why you lost the war in the first place." The assassin's eyes blazed, not with anger, but with the joy of victory. "Judge me all you want, but tonight Jons will offer me any woman who works for him, and I won't have to worry about money for months. You might have your honor, but at least I have a life."

"I'm going to enjoy killing you," Tomas said.

Aron laughed. "I bet you would. Unfortunately, I don't plan on giving you much of a chance." He leaned in closer. "It's your last offer. Tell me how you've lived so long without going mad. If you do, I'll give you a clean death."

Tomas smiled against the pain. "See, there's only one problem."

"What's that?"

"If you're not an honorable man, how can I trust you to keep your word?"

Aron's malicious grin was the last thing Tomas saw before the assassin's foot came down on Tomas' face.

27

T omas groaned as he came to, the sound harsh against his ears.

"How long have I been out?" he asked.

"Several hours," Elzeth replied. "It's nearly dawn."

Sounds of revelry snuck underneath the thick doors.

"It's been quite a party. You'd think that beating you and the knights was the equivalent of becoming king."

"I'm honored." He took a long, slow breath. "How am I?"

"Mostly healed. Though I'm tired. All your wounds are closed up, but some of them just barely. I spent a lot of time on your forearm, so if you do get something sharp in your hands again you'll be able to use it."

"Thanks."

"You're welcome. Now, I need to rest. Don't know what your odds of getting food here are, but if you can, that would be a big help."

Tomas nodded, and he felt Elzeth settle into a slumber.

He began by examining himself, as well as he was able. His hands were manacled behind his back, and his ankles were also connected by a length of chain bolted to the floor.

It wasn't nearly as restrictive as he'd feared, but he still wasn't going anywhere anytime soon. He was naked, so they'd found all his hidden knives. His clothes were in a pile off to the side, well out of reach. Even so, he doubted the Family was kind enough to lock him in here with his weapons.

He was in a bare room. From the sounds, Tomas guessed he was in the main gambling hall once again, on the first floor near the back, probably somewhere near the kitchens. He smelled old blood, and given the anchors in the floor, Tomas had some guess what the purpose of this room was.

He sighed, forcing himself not to think of the worse futures that might await him.

Life happened.

Sometimes, Family members with rifles snuck up behind you in the middle of a duel and shot you in the back. That was life. You could give into despair, or you could figure a way out.

Tomas tried to figure a way out. He tested the manacles, but they were tight and well secured. The chains around his ankles were the same. None seemed to have much in the way of give.

Not a promising start. A quick exploration of the anchor revealed that it, too, probably wouldn't give easily. He considered trying to kick at the wooden planks, but quickly dismissed that idea. Elzeth was near the end of his energy, and the most likely outcome was that he would attract attention and still be chained to the floor.

Perhaps a possibility for desperate times, but not yet.

Deciding there was no quick or easy way for him to escape, he made himself as comfortable as he could on the floor. The room had no windows, so there was no good way to tell the passage of the day. But he trusted Elzeth's sense of time. It was nearly dawn.

From the sounds of the activity in the hall, that didn't seem to matter much to the surviving Family members. Though there couldn't be more than a dozen left in total, they made enough noise to fool a listener into believing they numbered four times as many.

It didn't take long for there to be footsteps outside the door. The door opened and Tomas squinted against the bright light.

A lone figure stood silhouetted in the doorway. Tomas' eyes adjusted and he saw Mara, staring daggers at him and holding a knife in her hand to match.

She seemed hesitant, as though she stood on the edge of a cliff and she wasn't sure whether she should jump or turn around and save herself. Tomas remained still, concerned that anything he might do would be the piece that pushed her off the edge.

Then, with a strangled cry, she strode into the room. The speed of it caught Tomas by surprise, and Elzeth was too slow to wake. She stabbed at his heart, and all he could do was shift to the side, taking the knife into his right chest.

It was stopped by a rib, but it didn't hurt any less for not being fatal. Tomas bit down on the shout he wanted to release, refusing Mara the satisfaction. They could kill him, but they wouldn't break him.

For a second they were as close as lovers. He could smell the alcohol on her, could hear her sharp and short breaths. Her eyes widened slightly, and she stepped away, leaving the knife embedded in his chest.

She shook her head, as though she couldn't believe what she'd just done. She took another step back.

Had he not been distracted by the knife, Tomas realized

he had missed an opportunity. The boss' wife had come close enough to hurt and it hadn't occurred to him.

Mara turned and walked quickly from the room.

Tomas breathed deeply, trying to block out the pain. But with every breath the knife shifted, sending a new wave of agony to join the rest. And though the knife wasn't particularly deep, the blade didn't seem eager to leave its new home. Elzeth couldn't heal a wound with the knife still in it.

"At least she left you a knife," Elzeth said.

Tomas gritted his teeth, trying and failing not to chuckle. The knife wiggled some more, causing him to curse Elzeth. But the sagani spoke true. If he could get the knife out, he had options.

He groaned as he stood up. If he walked to the wall, he could probably knock the knife loose. He didn't relish the idea, but it was the first real opportunity he'd been given.

Before he could take a step, another shadow appeared in the doorway. Tomas glanced over and sighed.

Aron stood there, shirtless, one of Jons' women under his arm. The assassin smiled. "Saw her come in with a knife and leave without one. She didn't seem like the type, but I had to see for myself."

He lifted his arm off the woman and stepped in.

Tomas briefly considered fighting, but dismissed it. His only possible weapon was the knife in his chest, and it wouldn't do him much good. He was naked and bound. Even drunk as Aron no doubt was, it wouldn't be a fight.

It would be an excuse for Aron to kill him.

Aron looked disappointed. Then he shrugged, closed the last few paces to Tomas, and grabbed the knife. He worked it up and down a few times, slicing more of Tomas' chest. "Looks like she almost found the will. Maybe next time."

Aron pulled the knife out and tossed it into the hallway. Then he left, closing the door behind him as he groped at the woman who'd been keeping him company.

As soon as the darkness returned, Tomas let himself slump against the wall. His chest was bleeding freely, and he felt lightheaded.

"Lie down," Elzeth commanded.

Tomas did.

Elzeth went to work, but even Tomas could tell that the healing was slow. Elzeth was becoming exhausted, too.

"I'm not sure how much longer I'll be able to keep healing you," Elzeth admitted.

"I'll try my best not to get stabbed again," Tomas promised.

"You better. After this, I'm not sure how much use I'll be to you."

Tomas drifted off to sleep, Elzeth's final warning echoing in his thoughts.

28

His sleep was anything but dreamless. Once again, he was in a forest, although this one he could not name. This was something from Elzeth, from before they met. Elzeth had no names from the time before. He had possessed no thought, and in this dream memory, neither did Tomas.

Elzeth walked the steep mountain paths, soft paws silent as he stalked his prey. There was more space between the tall pines here, the forest diminishing as both predator and prey trekked ever higher.

He remained in cover as long as he could. When the opening came, he took it, bounding forward with long strides as he clenched his jaw on the smaller animal's neck. Two quick shakes snapped its neck, and Elzeth feasted, reveling in the warm meat as the body steamed in the cool mountain air. He had been hungry; now he no longer was.

Then he felt something, a presence somewhere down below, where the forest grew thicker. He looked up from his meal and stared down the mountain, searching for movement. He saw nothing.

But he was being watched. He felt it.

Only one creature hid itself so well. And if it was hiding, it knew of Elzeth.

The hunter became the hunted.

Elzeth finished his meal and ran, knowing the creature would eventually tire and abandon the pursuit.

As Elzeth ran, the dream faded to black.

Tomas blinked, then remembered where he was. The sagani had woken him, and when Tomas heard the pair of footsteps outside the door, he could guess why. The party, it seemed, was over. The hall was otherwise quiet.

Tomas grimaced as he sat up. His lips and throat were dry, and even sitting up felt like an impressive effort. Elzeth felt exhausted. He'd awoken Tomas and then started to drift back to sleep.

"How long?" Tomas asked.

"I'd guess it's about noon," Elzeth mumbled. Then he slumbered, so deep Tomas wasn't sure he'd wake if called. For the first time since Tomas had become a host, he felt truly alone.

Tomas couldn't see his chest where Mara had stabbed him, but it felt at least mostly healed.

The door opened and Tomas blinked again. Jons stepped inside. He carried a stool. He set the stool down, went back into the hallway, then brought back a lantern. One of his Family shut the door behind him.

Jons sat down on the stool, every motion planned and unhurried. He wanted Tomas to fear what was coming and gave that fear time to build. Tomas had never performed interrogations, but he knew that often the tortures prisoners imagined for themselves were just as effective as the actual torture.

Tomas noted that Jons sat well beyond the reach his

chains allowed. So he crossed his legs and waited for Jons to speak.

"You look terrible," Jons said.

"If you're concerned, a full meal and a hot bath wouldn't be unwelcome," Tomas said.

Jons grinned. "Good. I like a sense of humor in someone I'm questioning."

He paused, clearly waiting for the natural question in response. In other circumstances, Tomas wouldn't have given him the satisfaction. But he was tired and just wanted to get this over with. "Why?"

"Because humor is a defense. And a brittle one. It's what the weak hide behind when the world becomes too difficult for them to understand. It's a sign that you'll break easily."

"True enough," Tomas said. "Consider me broken. Ask your questions, and I'll answer them."

If Jons had hoped for more resistance, he didn't show his disappointment. "Why are you really here?"

"Told you the truth about that. I was just wandering through. Didn't plan on staying for more than a few days until your son started causing problems."

"I don't believe you," Jons said. "What are the odds a host would arrive right when the situation here was about to explode?"

"Slim," Tomas admitted, "but so it is."

"What do you want with the nexus?"

"To understand it."

From the expression on Jons' face, he still didn't believe Tomas. "You've gone to incredible lengths just to understand it. Why is it so important to you?"

Tomas looked around the room, wondering how much to tell Jons. "The church killed a lot of my friends. I believe the nexuses are important to the church. I want to know why. And if I can prevent the church from getting their hands on another one, I will."

"You accomplished that much," Jons admitted. "My scouts have already reported back from the nexus. Seems like my decision to help you wander out that way was a useful one. Now I control a nexus and four new rifles. So thank you."

"Four?" Tomas asked.

Jons smiled, sending a shiver down Tomas' spine. "Turns out they had more rifles than people willing to use them. Found a couple in the mission."

Tomas couldn't believe the news. There was no doubt left. Jons had won the town, and with it, the nexus.

"Why do you want it?" Tomas asked. "Why is it worth so much to the Family?"

Jons studied him for a moment. "You really don't know anything, do you?" He tapped his knee as he thought. Then he stood up. "You're a fool, Tomas."

Their interview, it seemed, was over. "Don't suppose you're going to let me go, now, are you?"

"I'm afraid not," Jons said. He paused, then spoke, his voice soft. It sounded like the boss was giving a confession. "I never had much love for Eiro. He was a boy who misunderstood power. He thought that being my son would give him some sort of protection, that he could do as he pleased and everyone would simply cower in fear. But in his heart, he was a coward who hid in my shadow, all the while acting as though he was the sun itself. I hated him for that."

Jons looked around the room. "But Mara loved that boy. I can't understand the love of a woman for her child, but so it is. Despite his very apparent flaws, she loved him. And he was our only child. We tried for others, but were never successful."

As Jons spoke, Tomas became more certain he was a dead man. These were the boss' private thoughts, words he'd likely never uttered to another soul. By saying them now, he guaranteed Tomas' end.

"You took everything from her when you took Eiro's life," Jons continued. "If I'm being honest, when I heard the news I was almost grateful. He was my son, yes, but he was a problem that I couldn't solve without dishonoring myself. But you killed the only hope Mara had for the future. I think it broke something inside of her."

A wicked knife appeared as if out of thin air, and Jons twirled it absently in his hand. "I'll torture you. Not because I hate you, but because I believe you know more than you're saying. If not about the nexus, about your own past. You were a host during the war, in one of the secret units that almost turned the tide. You know secrets, and secrets are worth an enormous amount of money in my trade. So I will get them from you.

"And when I am done, I will turn you over to Mara. Again, had it been me, I would have just killed you and been done with it." Jons turned to leave. He left Tomas with one last thought.

"Beware the wrath of a mother pushed too far."

After Jons left, Tomas slept. Worries filled his thoughts, but he had no ability to act on any of them. His body demanded rest and he obeyed.

His sleep was restless. Elzeth's memories, usually contained, leaked into his dreams.

The curse of the hosts. More strength than most humans could dream of, but whenever that strength was used, the barriers between host and sagani weakened. In time, the host either died or went mad. No host escaped the fate.

There was no harder skill to learn than restraint.

But restraint was what had kept Tomas and Elzeth alive as long as they had. As near as Tomas could tell, he'd outlived any of his peers by years.

Unfortunately, simple survival had demanded more from them over the course of the past day. Elzeth had expended enormous energies to keep him alive. But in doing so, he risked both Tomas' life and sanity.

His restless sleep ended shortly. Or at least, he assumed it had. His eyelids felt heavy and his body weak. He needed water and food. But somehow, he suspected Jons wouldn't be nearly the host Franz was.

He lay in the darkness, allowing his thoughts to wander. He battled the fear that crept into his worries, the premonitory chill that stole the warmth from his limbs. His memory of Jons, twirling the knife with such ease, grew until it was nearly all he could think of.

A voice broke him out of his growing fears. Tomas didn't recognize it, but it had come from just outside his door. There was another voice, this one more familiar, followed by the sounds of a scuffle.

The fight outside his door ended in a moment, when something that sounded an awful lot like a body flopped against the door.

Tomas heard the jingle of keys and then the lock turned. The door opened and one of the Family fell lifeless inside.

"You're a fool," Tomas croaked, but he couldn't stop a smile from spreading across his face.

"And you look like something I scraped off my shoe this morning," Franz answered. The innkeeper closed the door most of the way, leaving it open just a crack to let light through.

Tomas stood up, noticing how weak his legs felt. Franz brought over the keys and unlocked the manacles around his wrists and ankles. "Jons will kill you for this."

"He was going to kill us anyway. Takes me a while to get the obvious through my thick skull sometimes, but that's the truth of it."

Tomas held off on any further questions. Though he had plenty, they could wait until they were both in safer territory. He went to his clothes and put them on, noticing the number of cuts and holes that had been added to them in the past day. As he dressed, he asked Franz, "My sword?"

"There's a stash of weapons in the hall. Hold on." Franz stepped cautiously to the door, looked out, then disappeared for a moment. He reappeared with Tomas' weapons in hand. Tomas strapped them on quickly.

"That's a fair amount of steel," Franz observed dryly. "You worried you're ever going to stab yourself just sitting down?"

"The price of being well prepared."

Franz grunted, holding back his chuckle. Then he looked seriously at Tomas. "Will you be able to keep up?"

Any other day, Tomas would have been offended. Today he wasn't so sure he knew the answer. "Not much choice."

Franz nodded, then motioned for Tomas to follow. They exited the room, Tomas suppressing a shudder as he imagined the fate he'd just escaped.

Franz closed the door, locked it, then pocketed the keys. His grin was mischievous.

The gambling hall was otherwise silent. The celebration the night before had worn the Family out. Tomas saw that his guess about his room's location had been accurate. Franz led him through the kitchen and out the back door. Given the lack of bodies, Tomas assumed the route in had been unguarded.

They kept close to the walls of the buildings, the journey reminding Tomas of his first time sneaking from the hall to Franz's inn. Franz moved quickly and confidently, more than once having to wait for Tomas to catch up.

His stomach rumbled, his feet didn't want to obey his commands, and he was willing to kill for a drink of water. His vision swam as he stumbled behind the innkeeper. He constantly worried one of Elzeth's memories would consume his attention and he would be left standing motionless in the street like a drunken fool.

After several houses, Tomas gestured for a longer break. Tomas sagged when Franz stopped, his hands braced against his knees, barely remaining upright. He felt as though he'd run for days. "We can't go back to your inn. It will be the first place they look."

"We're not," Franz said.

Tomas heard Franz's sorrow. He could only guess how the loss of the inn would tear the innkeeper apart. But before he could utter his gratitude, Franz was supporting him. The old man remained wiry and strong.

"We need to keep moving. The Family controls both watchtowers now, and I think each one has a rifle. The longer we're outside, the greater the chance they find us."

Tomas nodded, too ashamed to admit he wasn't sure how much farther he could go on his own.

Franz continued supporting him, taking no small amount of Tomas' weight, never complaining once. They took a twisting route through the town but stopped sooner than Tomas expected. If he'd been given a map of town, he could easily point to where he was, but it meant nothing to him. The street was much the same as any other. It was quiet and residential. Franz knocked twice, paused, then twice more on a door.

The door slid open to reveal Inaya. Her red-rimmed eyes widened slightly when she saw them, and before Tomas could react, she was under his other arm, helping her grandfather support his weight.

The inside of the house was dark and cool, and reminded Tomas a little of Franz's inn. It possessed the same peace he'd come to associate with more traditional decor. But he couldn't focus on details. He felt safe within this house, and that was all that mattered.

They took him into a bedroom and laid him down.

Elissa came into the room and kneeled down beside him. He heard the sound of a ladle being dipped into water, and it was the most beautiful music he'd ever heard. Franz helped him lift his head and Elissa offered him a sip of water.

"Slow," Franz said.

Tomas obeyed, and the cool, clean liquid trickling down his throat sent a wave of relaxation through his body.

"Rest," Franz ordered him. "We should be safe until dusk. Then we'll use the cover of night to escape."

The whole family made to leave, but Tomas reached out and grasped the innkeeper's arm. Franz looked down at him.

"Thank you," Tomas said.

Franz bowed, then pulled himself free of Tomas' grip.

The family left, leaving Tomas alone.

A few seconds later, he surrendered to sleep.

30

T omas dreamed some of Elzeth's memories, but they were faint, like echoes of what they had once been. As both he and Elzeth slumbered, the barrier between them regained its shape and solidified. It allowed him to rest more easily and made his sleep worth the time.

When he woke again, it was to a soft knock on the door of his room. "Come in," he said.

Inaya entered, her head bowed. "Grandda said it was time to wake you. He's prepared supper, and it will be night soon."

If anything could convince Tomas to leave the comforts of his bed, it was another of Franz's meals. He sat up and noticed that a cup of water was next to him. He sipped the drink, savoring the cool liquid. "Thank you. I'll be there shortly."

She looked as though she might say something, but instead she bowed and exited the room.

Tomas stood and stretched. He ran through a single

empty-handed form, both to test his healing and his strength.

Neither were ideal. His wounds ached as the muscles and skin stretched and contracted. Elzeth's healing held, but Tomas wasn't in any condition to fight. The same went for his strength. He could walk and move without falling over, but he was pretty certain a duel between him and Inaya would be too close to bet safely on.

His stomach growled, reminding him he had more important matters to attend to. He left his room and followed his nose to the dining room. There he found Franz and his family seated around a round oak table, already passing out rice and beef.

A fourth place had been set for him, and he eagerly joined them. Elissa passed him warm bread, which he accepted with a small bow.

Tomas proceeded cautiously, but when his stomach didn't rebel too much, he started to eat faster.

"Thank you, again, for coming for me," Tomas said. "I can't believe you did."

Elissa snorted. "It was foolish, but I couldn't convince him otherwise."

Tomas smiled. Elissa might not have approved of Franz's actions, but she was proud of him all the same.

Franz took mock offense. "These old arms still have some strength in them, dear."

"They do," Tomas confirmed. "I listened when you attacked the guard. It was well done."

"Franz!" Elissa said, and Tomas flushed as he realized Franz had downplayed the extent of the danger of the rescue. He recalled then how little Elissa approved of violence, even for noble means.

The innkeeper looked sheepishly down at the table. All traces of the heroic rescuer vanished under his wife's glare.

Tomas came to his friend's aid. "You saved my life, and I will be forever in your debt."

Franz shook his head. "There is no debt between us. You saved Inaya, and then came and saved us from the mercenaries. If anything, the debt is still ours."

"There is no debt between friends," said Tomas. He looked at each member of the family. "But what caused you to change your mind about leaving?"

"Grandda finally realized how much danger we were in," Inaya said with a smile.

Franz grimaced. "Not exactly. I've always recognized the danger of staying. But it was always balanced by hope. Jons may not have a heart, but there's nothing wrong with his mind. There was no point in him being too aggressive, especially after the tributes we paid."

Franz cast his gaze down at the table. "Even after Eiro, I hoped that cooler heads would prevail. Perhaps it was a foolish hope, but I truly believed. But when I saw how they desecrated the knights, and when I heard they were planning on torturing you, it opened my eyes."

Tomas bowed again. "You'll always have my gratitude. It was bold, coming for me."

Franz waved away the compliment. "It was not so much. Their celebration could still be heard even when I woke this morning. I suspected they would be tired this afternoon. And Jons is spread thin. He doesn't have many Family left, and too many places to watch."

Tomas' admiration for the innkeeper continued to grow. He'd evaluated a dangerous situation rationally, which was no small feat. Only one question still intrigued him. "Whose house is this?"

Elissa answered. "A friend's. They already left town, as most have."

They finished their meal quickly while Franz sketched out their plan of escape. Once night fell they would leave town, following a route that largely kept them out of sight of the watchtowers. There was a chance they'd be spotted once they broke from the cover of town, but there wasn't much they could do about that. No escape was without risk.

Tomas looked at the family again. Of Inaya, he had few doubts. She was young and healthy. But for as much respect as he had for Franz, the innkeeper was well past the prime of his life. It was one thing to ambush a hungover guard. It was quite another to hike the endless miles of the prairie. And they would have to put many miles behind them if they hoped to escape the Family's pursuit. The Family had a long memory and longer reach. "Where will you go?"

"There's a place not too far from here," Franz said. "A little secluded place that's been abandoned for a year now. Maybe five miles away. We thought we might hide for a bit there, see how things end."

"You still think this might turn out in your favor?"

Franz shook his head. "It seems unlikely, but you're not dead yet, so the story isn't over. And one way or the other, these bones aren't traveling all the way back east. I've made that journey once and don't care to repeat it going the other way."

Tomas considered for a moment, but who was he to judge? "Long as it has a place to sleep," he said.

The meal ended and Franz's family went through the process of cleaning up. Tomas offered to help, but Elissa took one look at him and shook her head. "Rest while you can. You still look like a strong breeze would knock you over."

Tomas didn't argue. He watched the family clean and pack, their years of completing such tasks together giving them an easy familiarity. They danced around the kitchen and dining room as though the entire scene had been choreographed.

Tomas thought of his old squad, his friends now long dead, and the way they'd completed orders in much the same way. He felt the emptiness of their absence, a void he wasn't sure he'd ever be able to fill again.

If he could prevent such an emptiness for any of those three, he would. No matter the cost.

Soon they were ready. Franz opened the door and looked out. From Tomas' position behind the innkeeper, the street appeared quiet. Without Elzeth sharpening his senses, Tomas felt deaf and blind. But the sagani still slumbered, and Tomas didn't want to wake him unless he must.

They exited the house, with Inaya and Elissa so close behind Franz it almost looked as if they were embracing. Tomas followed a few paces behind, closing the door behind them.

Torches flickered in the direction of the main street, the moving shadows indicating the bearers of those torches were walking up and down the thoroughfare.

Franz led them farther away from the main street, following the path he'd outlined earlier. He only stopped when he heard his name called from the main street.

Tomas recognized Jons' voice, loud enough to be heard clearly even several houses away.

"Franz!" Jons called again.

Franz looked toward the center of town, then back to the edge.

Tomas gestured Franz toward the edge of town. Their only safety lay in that direction.

Franz whispered something to his wife and daughter, then made his way to the main street. As he passed Tomas, he said, "Might as well listen to what he's saying."

Tomas swore, but he couldn't leave the old man alone. He looked to the women, who reassured him with their gestures that they would stay in place. They, at least, had an ounce of reason. He followed the innkeeper.

Franz stopped in the shadows of the butcher shop, across the street from his inn and a building west. He poked his eye around the corner. Tomas did the same.

The Family didn't seem to be too interested in actually searching for Franz and Tomas. Instead, most of their forces had gathered in the main street, a circle of torches bright enough to turn dusk to day.

Jons, of course, was the center of attention, and literally stood at the center of the circle. Tomas searched for Aron but couldn't see him. He couldn't decide if that was good news or terrible.

Jons spun in a slow circle. When he spoke, it was loud enough to be heard, but not the call for attention he'd issued earlier. "Franz! I know you freed Tomas this afternoon. And I know you didn't make it far. So the choice is now yours. Will you turn Tomas over, or will you lose everything?"

Jons waited for an answer, a smile on his face.

Tomas sensed Franz's tension. The old man was contemplating stepping into the trap, and to the hells with the consequences.

"When I say everything, Franz, I mean everything," Jons said. "I'll start tonight with your inn, and if that isn't enough, I'll finish with your family. I'll let my Sons and Daughters do whatever they like to Elissa and Inaya, and you know they don't possess the same decency I do."

A few scattered hoots came from the crowd.

Jons reveled in it.

"I know you're out there somewhere, Franz. And trust me, Tomas isn't worth the loss of everything you love. I know you're an honorable man, Franz, so make the right choice here and we can let this all be in the past."

Beside him, Tomas felt the rage coming off the innkeeper.

Past his prime or not, Franz wasn't one to take an insult lying down.

Jons walked to the edge of the circle of Family, where he took a torch from one of his Daughters. He held it high. "Last chance, Franz. Turn Tomas over, or I burn your inn to the ground."

31

Tomas laid his hand on Franz's shoulder. The innkeeper was a mess of knotted muscles and barely restrained rage. Given Tomas' weakness, his gesture meant little. Franz could have twisted out of his grip with ease to confront Jons.

Franz quivered, no doubt torn between just that idea and saving his own life.

Tomas could do nothing but watch. He hadn't felt this helpless since he was a young man.

He hadn't *been* this helpless in that long.

All he could offer was his presence, and that seemed like pitifully little. His own anger rose, strong enough to stir Elzeth to the edges of awareness.

Jons waited for perhaps a minute, then walked over to Franz's inn. He broke one of the front windows and tossed the torch in. With a gesture from their boss, several of the other Family members followed suit.

Franz strained against Tomas' grip, but he didn't break it, though Tomas was certain he could have.

"I'll kill him," Franz whispered, voice on the verge of cracking.

"And I'll help," Tomas said, regretting the promise almost as soon as he'd made it. "But your wife and granddaughter need you now."

Franz tensed further, balanced on the edge of a precipice. Orange light flickered from inside the inn. For another minute, or perhaps a bit more, there was still a chance to save the building. A small group could conceivably rush in and extinguish the flames.

Then Franz sagged, as though he'd been punched in the stomach. He exhaled forcefully, then stood up straight, his shoulders relaxed. He blinked and tears trickled down his cheek. "I'd like to witness the end," he said.

Tomas watched the Family in the street, but they didn't seem too concerned about much of anything. He nodded.

The flames grew quickly, devouring the inn board by board. Franz watched until the fire had engulfed the entire structure, stretching high into the night sky, as though reaching for Tolkin.

Tomas kept the vigil with the innkeeper, unable to fathom what the older man experienced. He tried to imagine the hundreds of guests and the thousands of meals Franz had served over the years. Tried to imagine what it was like to watch a place he'd built with his own hands burn in less than an hour.

He couldn't. Place had no pull on him. One bed was as good as the other, and if no beds were available, he didn't mind a night under the stars. Home was wherever he was standing, and it didn't matter one bit to him. He mourned the loss of a peaceful place, but couldn't fathom the attachment that bound Franz to the inn.

The Family had to back up across the street, and Jons

directed a few to pour water on the nearby buildings. Even in his revenge, he was methodical. He ran this town, and only those who crossed him suffered the consequences.

Franz watched for a while, then stepped back, well out of sight of the Family, and bowed deeply toward the remains of his building. He held the bow for some time. Then he stood and nodded to Tomas. Together, the two of them returned to where they'd left Inaya and Elissa. Both women were in tears, and Elissa couldn't even find the strength to speak. The couple held each other closely while Tomas watched for Family.

Their mourning didn't take as long as Tomas expected. The old couple separated, and Franz once again led their way out of town. Just past the edge, they were forced to crawl for a ways, but there was no search for them. No one walked the grasses or called for them. As Franz had observed, Jons was spread too thin.

As soon as they were out of easy sight of the watchtowers, they stood and continued their journey.

Behind them, the flames of their former life could be easily seen. Tolkin cast the smoke from the fire in an eerie red glow that reminded Tomas too much of a bloodstained night sky.

They walked in silence. Franz and Elissa made the journey side by side, her smaller hand in his larger one.

In time, Inaya fell back so that she was walking next to him. She slowed her pace further and Tomas matched it, allowing them to distance themselves from the couple ahead.

"They amaze me," she said, her voice just soft enough to carry to his ears. "They've been together over forty years. They lost my mom, and gave up everything they had to make this journey out west. Now they lost that, and it still hasn't broken them."

"They're lucky to have one another."

"Yes, but they've also worked so hard to build their lives together. You know my grandma didn't want to move out west?"

Tomas shook his head. For the time he'd spent at their inn, and for the importance they'd come to have in his life, he knew next to nothing about them.

"Apparently they argued for months over it. Money was tight for them out east, but they were surviving. He had to work all the time, but they were comfortable enough. But he wanted more. To hear Grandda tell it, they argued all the way out here."

Tomas smiled at the thought.

"I want to have what they have," she confessed. She looked at him, and he saw what was in that look. With everything in her life uprooted, she was searching for something sturdy to hold onto.

And perhaps she thought he was what she was looking for.

She was a beautiful young woman. If anyone in town had caught Eiro's eye, he understood why it had been Inaya. And he was sorely tempted by her unspoken inquiry.

But she didn't desire him.

Not really.

She wanted stability, something she could anchor to in the tumultuous days to come. She saw that he kept his word, and that he still followed many of the old ways. To her mind, that meant he could be depended on.

Unfortunately, he wasn't what she needed. He wasn't even what she wanted, once she looked with clear eyes. He couldn't fulfill any of the promises she dreamed of.

"And someday, I believe you will," he said.

Her step faltered, but only for a moment. She didn't leave his side. Together they watched Franz and Elissa work their way through the prairie, their destination known only to Franz.

When the sun rose, they'd have to discover the next part of their lives together, but without Tomas.

32

They walked through a large portion of the night. Their unhurried pace would have troubled Tomas in other circumstances, but he was certain no one was searching the wilds for them yet.

Besides, he wasn't sure how much faster he could move. His body still ached.

At times, he felt as though he was one of Franz's family, a prodigal grandson returned from the wars, now wandering once again. He and Inaya would speak as though they had known each other for years. Then he would look at Franz and Elissa, holding hands, and knew he was a stranger among them.

Not long before Shen set on the eastern horizon, they came upon a small cabin. It was built near a grove of trees, and Tomas imagined water was close enough to the surface for a well. Its front window was shattered and the door hung open on its hinges, blowing softly in the wind.

Franz made straight for the structure, and Tomas was too tired to stop him.

"He's probably the strongest of us now, anyway," he grumbled softly.

Inaya, standing a few feet away from him, turned. "What?"

He shook his head. "Just talking to myself."

Franz approached the cabin cautiously, although Tomas didn't see the point. If the cabin was occupied, those within had already seen them. But he guessed it was unlikely anyone slept within. They would have at least shut the door.

The innkeeper poked his head through the door, then motioned them forward.

Tomas was the last to enter, and by the time he did, the cabin was already a hive of activity. Elissa had found a broom and was sweeping the floor while Inaya and Franz searched for something among their carried goods to cover the broken window with.

The cabin certainly lacked the amenities Tomas had come to enjoy in Franz's inn. It had only the one room, with an old small wood stove in the corner. Tomas decided to make himself useful and search for wood.

He found a small pile on the back side of the cabin. Whoever had lived here had even built a small protective covering for the wood, so it was nice and dry. He brought enough back to warm the cabin for the rest of the night and into the early morning.

By the time he returned, the cabin had been cleaned into a livable condition. The place was far from luxurious, but it was safe enough for the moment, and it was a roof over their heads. Their bedrolls had been laid out, including Tomas'.

The others fell asleep almost immediately, their soft snores slowly filling the cabin. Tomas lit the fire and tended it for a bit, his thoughts bound up in the flickering flames. But he was also exhausted and needed rest. "You awake enough to keep watch?" he asked.

"I am," Elzeth said. The sagani sounded like he'd just stirred from a long nap and hadn't fully awakened. Still, just hearing his voice reassured Tomas.

"You sure?"

"Get some rest," Elzeth said. "I'll be fine."

"Don't worry about healing or anything like that," Tomas said. "I think we have some time."

Elzeth grunted, annoyed that Tomas was still talking.

Tomas followed orders and went to sleep. For once, it was deep and dreamless.

He woke to the others beginning their daily chores. Elissa had water boiling for tea, and it sounded as though Franz was busy over the stove. Whatever he was cooking, it smelled wonderful.

Over a surprisingly delicious breakfast, they debated their next actions. After the loss of his inn, even Franz admitted that it was time for them to move on. He'd held on to his losing hand for as long as possible, hoping his fortune might change. But there was nothing left.

Tomas finished breakfast admiring the family even more. The pain in their decision was easy to see. Although he couldn't quite empathize, he could mourn what they had lost, and he recognized the challenges still ahead.

Such a disaster would break many. Tomas could name, almost without having to think about it, a dozen individuals who had cracked and fallen into despair over less. But Franz and Elissa had steel in their spines. No matter how many blows they endured, they kept their eyes focused clearly on the work ahead.

And he saw how. He noticed how Franz and Elissa sat so close they brushed against the other whenever they moved. He saw Franz's eyes twinkle when they settled on Inaya. And Inaya, for her part, doted on whatever need of her grandparents she noticed.

Their inn was lost, but their family was not. And it was clear which mattered most to each of them.

The only point of contention was how soon to move. Franz wanted to wait a day. He had a friend who farmed outside a town about twenty miles distant. Franz believed the friend would be willing to ferry them to Tansai, where they could begin their lives anew.

Tomas wanted them to move faster. He couldn't predict what Jons would decide in regard to Franz and his family, but he didn't want to stick around to find out.

Franz, though, believed that Jons' burning of their inn would satisfy the boss, at least temporarily. He wanted to rest for a day, and thought they were safe.

In the end, Franz won.

The innkeeper was probably right. Jons had more important problems than Franz. He needed to secure the town and the nexus, and he didn't have many Family to do so with.

While the others rested in the cabin, Tomas went out into the grove of trees. He didn't do well sitting for long periods of time, nor did he feel like resting. His limbs still felt heavy, and he needed more sleep, but the events of the past few days had left him with a simmering anger.

Tomas found a clearing in the grove and practiced his forms. At first he was slow, his movements more uncoordinated than he was used to. But after a few repetitions, the exhaustion fell from his limbs. Once he'd worked up a slight sweat, he changed the focus of his practice.

His thoughts were on Aron. Specifically, on the techniques Aron used.

The assassin was faster than him. He'd proven that decisively. His technique was built on that speed, linear attacks that minimized the time an opponent had to react.

Tomas ran through different scenarios, practicing the techniques he might reply with in the small clearing. Nothing seemed promising. The combination of Aron's skill and sagani-assisted strength seemed an insurmountable obstacle.

The snap of a twig broke his concentration. He glanced up to see Inaya approaching.

"Sorry to interrupt," she said. "I was just getting bored in the cabin. They're discussing logistics and plans, and I just can't think that far ahead, not yet."

Tomas sheathed his sword. "It's no problem. A break would probably do me some good."

"What will you do next?"

"Escort you to your grandfather's friend."

"And then?"

"Haven't decided."

"Are you going to attack them?"

"Haven't decided."

"But you're considering it?"

He paused, then confessed, "I am."

"You should just leave. Continue out west. There's no point in risking your life any further. We'll be safe."

Tomas scratched at his chin. He'd thought of doing the same. As much as he wanted justice for Franz and his family, and as much as he wanted to protect the nexus, both ideals were out of reach and dangerous. Perhaps it was far wiser to leave this all behind and continue his journey.

But the idea of leaving grated at him, like leaving an

open wound without a bandage. Jons had wronged an innocent family, and there was still a knight commander somewhere out there who needing killing. The idea that such behavior would go unpunished sickened him, and would bother him no matter how many miles he put between him and this cursed town. He saw that Inaya was waiting for some kind of answer. "I'll take it under advisement," he said.

"You better," she said. "I'll leave you to your training, though."

"Don't wander too far," he cautioned.

She waved her hand dismissively, but he expected she would listen. She was young, but she wasn't a fool.

After she was gone, Elzeth stirred to life. "You could do far worse in this world than her."

"True, but I'd bring her no joy."

Elzeth was silent for a few seconds, but Tomas knew he had more to say. "You can't beat Aron. Not like this."

"I know."

"So what's it going to be? I know you won't just walk away. Which leaves only death or unity."

"I know." His mouth was suddenly dry. "Do you think we can handle it?"

"I get the feeling you're not going to leave us with much choice."

"Tell me no and I'll walk away. You have my word."

Elzeth considered for some time. "You'd be a pain to live with. I'm with you, even if it comes to that."

They trained for a while longer, but focus was impossible to find. Eventually, they called it quits. With another full night of rest, he hoped that he would be close to full strength once again. He returned to the cabin and alternated napping with helping plan the family's trip. They ate another meal together, and that night Tomas fell into a deep and contented slumber.

He woke to Franz stirring him awake, the sun still not risen.

"It's Elissa," he said. "She left this morning and hasn't come back. I'm worried something happened to her."

33

Tomas questioned Franz closely, quickly getting the truth of the story despite the innkeeper's agitation.

Elissa was by nature an early riser. Franz and Inaya were the two often responsible for the inn late in the evening. This morning she'd woken early, much like any other. She'd remained in bed for a while out of deference to the others, but quickly grew bored with the lack of activity. She and Franz had whispered together, and had agreed that perhaps it would be a good idea to search the surrounding area for herbs or other usable goods for their trip.

Franz confessed he hadn't expected much from the excursion. More than anything, he'd felt that Elissa wanted to stretch her legs and have some small bit of time alone. She agreed to remain close to the cabin and promised to be back by dawn.

And now the sun had risen and Elissa still hadn't returned.

Franz had searched the nearby area and found nothing.

"Elzeth?" Tomas asked his sagani.

"He speaks true. It didn't seem worth it to wake you."

Tomas frowned. The sagani had made the decision so he could rest, and the time had been needed. He wanted to be angry at Elzeth, but the truth was, even had he woken up, he probably would have agreed to the plan. Perhaps it hadn't been the safest course of action, but neither would it have felt particularly foolish.

And anyway, from Elzeth's tone, there was already enough regret to go around.

Tomas didn't bother to placate Franz with empty promises that everything would be okay. No one in the cabin believed for a moment that Elissa was safe. She was too responsible to have forgotten the time or to have gotten lost or hurt in the predawn darkness.

No, if she hadn't returned, someone had prevented her from doing so.

Tomas cursed himself. He'd let Franz convince him this cabin was a safe place to rest. But it was too close to town. Of course someone would think of it as a hiding place. And Elissa had paid the price for his foolishness.

Tomas told the others to wait in the cabin while he explored. They protested, but he cut them off before they could finish their arguments. Either they stayed by his side and slowed him down, or they remained here where he could at least know where they were.

Franz clenched his fists, but acquiesced.

Tomas opened the door and looked out. The sun had just crested over the horizon, the early morning orange hues of sunrise fading to pale blue. He let his eyes wander over the surroundings, Elzeth sharpening his senses. His body still felt tired, but he was healed and ready to fight.

As near as he could tell, no one watched the cabin. It was the threat of the rifles he worried about the most. Not for himself, but for Franz and Inaya. Bullets would rip through the walls of their hideout without difficulty.

"Ready?" he asked Elzeth.

The sagani stirred to life in response.

Tomas turned to the others. "I'll be back soon."

Without waiting for a response, he sprinted from the door. He heard Inaya gasp, then he was out in the prairie.

It would take one of the world's best shooters to hit him moving at speed, and he used that speed to make a circle around the cabin, even darting in and among the grove of trees to search for enemies.

Once he was reasonably certain no one waited for them outside the cabin, he returned to the front door and began searching for tracks. The area around the cabin was trampled, but it helped that they hadn't strayed too far since their arrival.

He found his and Inaya's footprints from their trip to the grove the day before. After a while, he found another set, mostly partial prints barely visible. He couldn't identify them for sure as Elissa's, but they appeared fresh. They followed a well-worn game trail.

He pursued the trail, not sure it was Elissa's, but lacking many better options.

She'd stopped at a few clumps of wildflowers that had healing properties, which made Tomas think he was on the right track. She had been searching for anything that might be useful on their upcoming journey.

His stomach clenched as he came over a small rise and dropped to the other side. Now, for the first time, he was out of sight of the cabin. He worried he would find Elissa's body, cold and pale in the grass.

He breathed out a sigh of relief when he found the signs of a struggle. Several sets of footprints led away, back in the direction of town. Tomas followed them for a few minutes, wondering if he might catch up to them before they reached the protection of the Family-owned town.

His pursuit came to naught. After he crested another small rise he saw a place where a group of horses had trampled the grass.

He thought about pursuing further, but thought better of it. They knew what he was, and they would move quickly. Given their lead, he didn't think he could catch them before they reached the protection of the rifles.

And Aron.

Tomas ran back to the cabin.

Though his news was bad, there was hope. He felt good. He'd pushed his body and Elzeth, and neither had given any sign of weakness. And he hadn't found Elissa's body.

He reached the cabin, and in response to Franz's questioning gaze, he shook his head. "She's been taken back to town. I think there was a group of them watching the cabin overnight."

Inaya began to cry, and Franz grabbed at Tomas. "You need to save her!"

"I will," Tomas said. He looked out at the sky and grimaced. There would be no sneaking up on the town in the daylight. "I'd like to wait until nightfall, though."

Franz shook his head. "They'll kill her."

"They won't. If she's dead, there would be no reason for me to come. And it's me Jons wants dead most of all." Tomas didn't worry that they would kill Elissa. But his unspoken concern was that the Family would still harm her.

He swore to himself and sat in the corner, trying to ignore Franz's desperate looks. He also didn't like the idea of waiting until night, but it was the easiest way to deal with the rifles.

Tomas set himself to thinking. Against just Aron or just the rifles, he might have tried a daylight assault. Against both, he didn't see a way to safely reach town. But every time he looked at Inaya and Franz, beside themselves with worry, he reconsidered. Perhaps it was worth the risk.

Elissa was tough, though. He had to believe she was strong enough to handle any punishments Jons might invent.

Then he thought of Mara and his blood turned to ice.

Tomas stood and paced. Perhaps it wasn't wise to wait. He was assuming everyone in the Family would be rational. But there was no guarantee of that.

In the end, his decision was made for him.

Inaya stepped outside the cabin and called for them a few moments later. Franz and Tomas joined her. Her finger pointed in the direction of the town. A thick plume of black smoke rose into the air.

Something in the town was on fire.

34

Tomas watched the smoke billow ever higher. Without a wind it simply rose, wide and dark against the otherwise blue sky. It was no signal fire, nor even a lone building lit to attract their attention.

Given the amount of smoke, at least a few buildings were burning.

Something more was happening.

He turned to the other two. From their determined looks, he realized it would be pointless to ask them to remain behind. But at the same time, he couldn't wait for them. "I'm going ahead," he said. "Be careful when you approach."

Franz nodded.

With that, Tomas once again faced the town. He queried Elzeth, who signaled his readiness. The sagani was the more cautious of the two of them, but even he had nothing to say now. He didn't even suggest they retreat.

Tomas ran, pacing himself carefully. Hosting a sagani was an artform, a constant balance between the strength the creature offered and the madness it promised. Fortunately, they had years of experience balancing on that particular tightrope.

He bounded across the prairie at what most humans would consider a full run, his pace eating up the miles. He and Elzeth could run this fast all day and still arrive ready to fight at the battlefield.

Flashes of great ironwood trees, taller than the watch-towers in town, seared fresh images in his memory. They didn't last a second, but they reminded him the barriers between him and Elzeth remained weak.

"We haven't done anything like this in years," Elzeth said.

"Miss it?"

"Not particularly."

Tomas laughed.

"Say what you will," Elzeth observed, "but there's a part of you that wanted this."

Tomas' laughter faded. But his hair blew in the wind and his footsteps were light and fast. His sharp gaze caught sight of a wild sagani off to the east, traveling in the direction of the nexus. His nose picked up the scent of blooming flowers.

Only crisis made reality so vivid. He told himself he didn't like to fight, but maybe that wasn't the whole truth.

Perhaps he wasn't made for peaceful times.

The thought troubled him.

He ran faster, outrunning the thought and all others as he neared the town. Now that he was closer he could hear the sound of rifles from at least two different locations.

People were shooting at one another.

Tomas slowed as the town came into view. It looked like it was under siege. The source of the fire was easy enough to spot. One of the watchtowers was gone, devoured by flames.

It looked like when it collapsed it had fallen on several houses, which now also burned.

Elzeth helped him focus on the shapes moving in town. The same citizens who hadn't bothered to help him when he'd been shot were now out trying to save their homes.

His heart didn't go out to them. He understood the desire for self-preservation as well as the next wanderer, but in the whole town, only Franz and his family had ever shown him kindness. When the others had seen him bleeding and alone on the streets, not one had offered to help.

Tomas watched the houses burn and decided he would return the lack of assistance.

He looked for signs of Elissa. If Jons' intent was to draw him in, she'd be somewhere visible.

His guess proved correct. She stood near a pole that had been erected outside of Jons' gambling hall. Her wrists had been tied behind her back and then pulled upward by a length of rope which attached to the pole.

Thankfully, her feet remained firmly on the ground. Had she been suspended in a true strappado, he didn't think she would still be alive. All the same, the position had to be tremendously painful.

His hand went to his sword as another volley of rifle shots rumbled over the plains.

He broke his gaze from Elissa to look around. He spotted a figure, standing alone in the prairie. The man held a rifle and fired into town. Tomas couldn't say for sure, but it appeared as though he was firing at the second watchtower.

The watchtower was firing back, but the figure in the distance shifted position too rapidly to track. Tomas focused on the figure, his heart racing as he understood what he was seeing.

The town was under siege.

A siege of one man.

The man fired his rifle three more times, each time shifting position after he fired.

Tomas almost wondered why Aron didn't come out, but that question was answered easily enough. His opponent had a rifle and the reflexes to kill a host. With much of Aron's speed meaningless, it made no sense for him to leave cover. Eventually, the man would have attack in person. And when he did, Aron would be there to collect his head.

Tomas' eyes drifted over to Elissa, suspended in the middle of the chaos. "Hells."

Elzeth, resigned to what was to come, found his dry humor once again. "You didn't want to get old anyway."

"Guess not."

The man besieging the town dropped his rifle, as Tomas had known he eventually would. For all their abilities, rifles were still constrained by ammunition. But a sword never ran out of bullets. And this was a man who would want to get in close, to feel the blood of his enemies against his face.

The man sprinted forward, his speed inhuman.

Tomas squatted, waiting to see how the situation developed. He didn't like leaving Elissa in the center of danger, but he trusted she would survive for a while yet.

The watchtower fired its rifle at the man, but he moved too quickly, his advance too random to aim ahead of him. The man entered town, and only a few moments later, Tomas saw the whole watchtower shake as one of its supports was cut.

He now had a pretty good guess what had happened to the first one.

A few seconds later, the watchtower collapsed. It fell in the direction of Jons' gambling hall, and while it was too far away to crush the den of thieves, it did destroy several houses.

Not long after that, Tomas heard the echoing clang of steel rise up from the town. The battle had been joined in earnest. Aron had joined the fight.

He stood.

He breathed deeply, allowing Elzeth to spread more throughout his body. His fingers tingled and the energy became overwhelming. He wanted to run. He needed to run, needed to act. The act of thinking became difficult.

But one thought remained clear.

The knight commander hadn't just escaped a couple of nights ago. He'd run for the nexus, fought a sagani, and became the one thing he hated most in the world. The thing he had spent most of his life hunting. For revenge, he'd sacrificed his own soul.

The knight commander was now a host, and he'd returned for revenge.

35

W ith the collapse of the watchtower, Tomas decided not to wait any longer. On the other side of town, the fires continued to spread. The wind was slowly picking up, and despite the efforts of the townspeople, the fire wouldn't be halted. The town was a corpse that didn't realize it was dead yet.

He needed to recover Elissa before it was too late.

His legs covered the last of the distance to the town with little problem. Thanks to the loss of the watchtowers and the fight happening outside Jons' hall, there was no one watching the prairie for him. He made his way to the houses at the edge of town without being observed.

Unlike most of his journeys through town, he made no effort to hide. He stuck to smaller side streets. Several houses over he could hear the duel between the hosts, and he had no desire to take part.

Not until Elissa was safe.

He heard the group of Family before he saw them. Three pairs of feet, stepping heavily between the houses.

They were in his way. He turned the corner, surprising them all.

He barely slowed.

His sword cleared its sheath, tracing a path through his enemies. He snapped the blood off his blade and sheathed the sword again. Not a single Family had managed to so much as get their sword up in response.

He was well past them by the time their bodies hit the ground.

Then he was behind Jons' gambling hall, near the back entrance that connected to the kitchen. He didn't have any particular desire to visit this place again, considering how he'd been hosted on his last visit. But it provided cover from the duel happening on the other side of the building.

So through the hall it was.

And anyway, if he had to clear out a few Family on the way, the world would be better for it.

He opened the back door and stepped into the kitchen. One Daughter was there, packing up food supplies. She looked up and her mouth formed an "O" when she saw who it was. She reached for a knife sitting next to her, but by the time her hand touched it, Tomas had already cut through her neck.

He left the kitchen and came into the hallway. He startled a Son carrying a crate of goods.

Tomas left a throwing knife embedded in his forehead as he passed.

The main hall was full of activity when he entered, and he imagined that almost every surviving Family member was here. He counted six, including Mara, who was behind the bar selecting bottles to bring with them.

Mara saw him first, and her eyes went wide as she

screamed. That caught the attention of everyone, who turned and noticed him.

They drew swords and attacked.

Tomas ran, jumping up first onto one of the card tables and then leaping into the crowd. His sword led the way, and he soon found himself surrounded by the last of Jons' Family. He cut through them, careful not to lose focus as he did.

The confined spaces worked to his advantage. He twisted around tables and kicked chairs at his opponents, giving himself easier one-on-one fights that he won decisively.

The entire time he kept half an eye on Mara. She had climbed over the bar and was now on the other side, kneeling over one of the fallen Family.

For a moment, Tomas thought she might be trying to comfort a Son, or provide him aid.

But she wasn't.

All she took from the dying man was his sword.

Had she possessed any wisdom at all, she would have run. She knew what he was. But her eyes shone brightly as she picked up the weapon and pointed it in Tomas' direction. The tip wavered and her grip on the hilt was anything but firm. She'd never even held a sword before, but still she advanced.

Tomas killed the last of the Family with a dismissive cut, then turned to Mara.

She came at him, slow but steady, without even a hint of hesitation.

Tomas caught movement out of the corner of his eye, from up high. He glanced up and saw Jons, holding a rifle. For the first time since they'd met, Tomas thought he saw a true emotion on the man's face.

It was fear.

"Mara!" he called.

He raised the rifle, bringing it to his shoulder. At the same time, Mara raised her sword, the action unbalancing her.

Tomas stepped forward and offered Mara an everlasting peace. The rifle went off, but Jons hadn't had time to aim. The bullet passed safely behind Tomas.

Mara's head fell to the floor, followed a few moments later by her body.

Tomas looked up at Jons, the boss' face twisted in agony, his gaze focused on his wife's corpse. Whatever disagreements they may have had, he had loved her. She'd been fire to his ice, and as he watched, the cold exterior he'd worked so hard to maintain finally melted.

His eyes traveled over to Tomas, who coldly flicked Mara's blood from his sword.

Jons snarled and twisted, the muzzle of the rifle snapping toward Tomas. Tomas waited until he could stare down the bore, then moved. Jons' finger tightened on the trigger, and a second later Tomas watched the bullet pass through the space he'd just stood.

Tomas jumped up onto a card table, then at the railing of the stairs that led up to the balcony. Jons tracked with the rifle, able to shift his aim even faster than Tomas could move.

Tomas ran two steps up the railing, his balance making the narrow strip of wood feel as wide as the town's main street. When Jons' aim caught up to him, he jumped from the railing, Elzeth's strength allowing him to leap all the way to the balcony.

Jons fired again, but Tomas was no longer where Jons expected him to be. Again the bullet was nowhere near him.

Jons twisted the other way, trying to bring the rifle back on target, but Tomas was too fast. He landed on the balcony and made a sweeping cut, slicing through the heart of the blasphemous weapon. Jons took a step back as he dropped the rest.

He made no cry, nor asked for mercy.

He'd been a soldier once, and from his reaction, Tomas knew he'd faced death before.

Tomas remembered the first time he'd met the boss, the sense of kinship they had shared. Even Franz had said that Jons had managed the town fairly. He held back the final cut. "Draw your weapon," he said.

Jons sneered. "So you can feel better about yourself when you kill me?"

"So you can have the honor of dying with your sword in hand."

A complex set of emotions played across Jons' face at Tomas' words. His sneer lasted for another second or two, but then the meaning of Tomas' proposal seemed to hit him with full force. He struggled to accept the offer, but after a few seconds, his cool demeanor returned.

Jons straightened, then brushed some imaginary dust from his clothes. He looked Tomas in the eye and offered a short bow. Tomas bowed his head a fraction of an inch in response. It was the most he could offer the boss.

Jons shifted his position. He brought one foot back and lowered his weight. His hand went to the hilt of his sword, gripping it with the confidence born of experience. Then he waited.

Tomas recalled that Jons was known as an excellent swordsman. But he didn't doubt his choice.

He respected Jons' choice of technique. A sword draw was a clean way to end this battle. He sheathed his own sword and mirrored Jons' stance. He breathed easily, waiting for the decisive moment.

Jons gritted his teeth, knowing he was staring at his final moments. In the street out front, two swords clanged together, which served as signal enough for Jons. He attacked.

With Elzeth's aid, Tomas saw Jons' body tense the moment before he began to move. At the first sign of that tension, Tomas drew his sword.

They both made their cuts.

But it wasn't close.

Tomas snapped the blood of the last of the Family off his blade and sheathed it.

The swords clanged again outside.

The real battle was yet to begin.

36

Tomas stepped out the front door of the gambling hall and into one of the three hells.

In the time it had taken him to clear the hall, chaos had seized the town. Tomas didn't see either of the hosts in the street, but the sound of their swords meeting echoed in the air. The fire had spread rapidly, though, with several more houses now on fire. Those few in the town who still lived tried helplessly to slow the flames, but with the wind now gusting, there was no chance. Homeowners threw buckets of water on buildings, but they might as well have tried to dam a river with a handful of sticks.

Tomas ran over to where Elissa hung. He put his shoulder under her so that the sudden shift in her weight wouldn't worsen her suffering, then cut through the rope with a knife. Her bound wrists fell and she groaned in pain.

"Don't move," Tomas said, and he used the same knife to cut through the ropes binding her wrists. When the last rope snapped, Elissa cried out. Her arms flopped to her side, lifeless. Tomas hoped it was just a lack of blood to the limbs, but he didn't have time to examine her closely. They could have been dislocated or broken, but those injuries hardly mattered now.

"I'm going to pick you up and get you out of here," Tomas said.

Footsteps, too quick to be human, sounded close behind him. They were the only warning he had. He dove forward, pulling Elissa with him, twisting to take as much of the impact as he could. A sword flashed in the sunlight above him as they fell.

The impact caused Elissa to utter another cry, but Tomas couldn't spare her any attention. He pushed himself to his feet in time to see the knight commander ready himself for another attack.

It was the first time he'd seen the knight commander up close since the battle several days ago. The man's pupils were dilated and thin red lines snaked around the edges of his eyes. His breathing was fast and shallow, and Tomas could even hear the pounding of the knight's heart, beating nearly twice as fast as Tomas' own.

"Hells, he's burning fast," Elzeth said, concern and despair in his voice. For a sagani was the source of that power, one that would soon be dead, regardless of the outcome of the duel.

"You're not going anywhere, demon!" the commander shouted. He attacked again, his speed incredible.

But the knight lacked control. The sagani inferno that raged within him gave him more strength and speed than he'd ever known, but he hadn't yet learned to harness the power. Like an unbroken stallion, he had strength to spare, but no direction to travel, no guidance or focus.

Tomas slid out of the way as the knight passed him. The attack carried the commander a good fifteen feet past him.

Tomas looked around the burning town. Despite the

knight's inexperience, Tomas couldn't get Elissa to safety while fighting the knight.

The situation worsened when Aron found his way back to the street. He grinned when he saw Tomas. "Look who showed up! Don't we just have ourselves a fun little gathering here?" He casually whipped a throwing knife at Elissa, as though he was playing some sort of bar game, but Tomas sliced at the weapon and sent it off its course.

"No fun," Aron pouted. "No fun at all."

The knight, apparently frozen by the choice of which demon to kill first, looked between the two of them. Aron glanced over at the man. "Of course, he's even less fun."

The verbal jab was designed to antagonize, and it succeeded. The knight rushed at Aron, and the two met in the middle of the street. The knight's speed almost matched Aron's, and with each pass he learned how to control his newfound abilities a bit better.

Their blades danced around one another, meeting twice, filling the street with the now familiar sound of steel on steel.

Tomas backed up until he was next to Elissa. If the two other hosts remained engaged, perhaps he would have enough time to escort her away.

The knight suddenly lost his footing and came flying backward at Tomas, kicked by Aron with incredible force in the chest. Tomas ducked and the knight passed overhead, cursing all the time.

Aron shook his head. "Such poor language from a man of the church, don't you think, Tomas?"

The assassin came at Tomas, covering the space between them in less than a heartbeat.

Tomas slid away from Elissa, preventing Aron from cutting at her. They stabbed at each other, neither finding the opening they sought. Where Aron and the knight's duel was characterized by the clashing of swords, this was defined by the whisper of their blades through the air.

Their duel didn't last long. The knight regained his feet and joined the melee, breaking Tomas and Aron apart as they each had to deal with the new threat.

Alliances were made and broken in instants, a series of rapidly shifting two-on-one fights. But both Aron and the knight had a tendency shift sides without warning, whenever they saw an opening in their temporary ally's defense.

With every pass, the knight also improved. His skill couldn't match either Aron's or Tomas', but the gap narrowed quickly. The church didn't bestow knighthood on fools, and the commander would have been among the best of the knights to earn his title. Tomas feared if the battle continued for much longer, he would face two terrifying opponents.

To top it off, he couldn't move Elissa, nor did she seem inclined to escape on her own. She hadn't so much as stirred since he'd landed hard with her to avoid the knight's attack.

The three hosts exchanged another flurry of cuts, but they were effectively stalemated. No one host was strong enough to defeat two, but no two could band together long enough to defeat one.

When they broke apart again, Tomas saw Inaya, hiding near the corner of Jons' gambling hall.

Her presence changed his options. Their eyes met, and he gave her a brief nod.

Then he ran. When he neared the knight, instead of fighting, he jumped. His leap took him well out of the knight's reach, and when he landed behind the knight he kept running farther into town. The knight cursed and chased after him, gaining ground quickly.

Aron followed, likewise closing the gap with every step. Tomas risked one glance behind him, wondering how much space he could give Inaya. He saw the girl running toward Elissa.

The knight caught up to him not far from where Franz's inn had once stood. It was now nothing but smoldering ruins. But it wouldn't be alone for long. The church side of the town was a raging inferno, every building on fire.

Tomas pivoted on a heel and met the knight, surprising him with the sudden move. He scored a gash along the knight's thigh, but his rush of satisfaction vanished when he saw that Aron had stopped following. The assassin had given up the chase, turned, and was watching Inaya help Elissa to her feet.

Tomas slid around the knight's attack, most of his focus on Aron. Would the assassin fight the hosts, or would he kill the women?

Tomas parried a thrust from the knight, his attention torn between the threats.

Which would it be?

His heart sank as Aron walked away from the duel and toward the women.

37

Tomas turned to pursue Aron, but the failure of his plan quickly became evident. The knight demanded his full attention, attacking with a quick series of cuts that made him give up ground.

Now Elissa and Inaya were alone against Aron, and there was only one way that battle ended.

Tomas tried to break away from the knight, but again the knight stopped him.

Fortunately, Aron was taking his time. He walked slowly down the street, savoring his moment of triumph. Even so, Tomas didn't have long.

He had to deal with the knight.

The knight attacked again, and this time Tomas met him. Their blades crossed and rang out. Tomas pushed the knight back several steps, but couldn't find an opening. The knight was burning too hard and learning too fast.

They broke apart, and the knight took a few extra steps back. He blinked rapidly, as though trying to clear something from his vision. He pressed his left palm against his forehead and grimaced.

Tomas knew those signs well enough. Tics. The first signs that madness was setting in, the boundaries between warrior and sagani dissolving into nothingness. The knight couldn't have been a host for more than a few days. To be so far gone — it was unheard of.

"He's been burning that hard since the first moment they joined," Elzeth said.

There was no way of knowing, but the assumption rang true. Tomas couldn't imagine any other way of falling so far so quickly.

He felt no sorrow for the knight. The commander had spent his life hunting hosts, had led others in the same quests. When Tomas noticed the tics, he attacked.

The knight saw and moved, his response almost too quick for Tomas to catch. Tomas' cut missed wide, the knight no longer where he was supposed to be.

Tomas twisted, but too slowly.

The knight unleashed an assault of steel equal to at least three trained warriors. Tomas deflected, dodged, and gave up ground as fast as his balance would allow. But the knight's sword was like a three-headed snake. Tomas would block one strike only to see the sword coming at him from another direction. The knight found impossible openings, the blade coming ever closer to Tomas' vital organs. Cuts appeared on Tomas' arms, chest, and legs.

"Look at me!" the knight shouted, all semblance of the calm commander Tomas had once known gone. "I've become a demon, just like you!"

Tomas' only response was to retreat further. The commander was driving him deeper into the church's side of town, now one raging fire that ran from the north side of town to the west. Heat scorched his back, and every pace took him farther from the people he'd sworn to protect.

"Bathe in the waters of your everlasting redemption!" the knight cried. He pressed his advantage. There wasn't much space for Tomas left to give. Soon he'd be walking into the flames.

"Tomas," Elzeth said. "It's time."

Tomas grimaced. They'd spoken about it, but the idea still caused his knees to shake. He needed no more reason than to look at the knight. What Elzeth proposed wasn't much different. Except they would assume the risk with full knowledge and by choice.

Off in the distance, Aron was only twenty paces away from Elissa and Inaya. The two women had reached their feet, but they couldn't possibly outrun the assassin.

"Okay," he said.

And he surrendered.

He dropped the barriers he'd spent so long developing and maintaining, and what little separation existed between him and Elzeth vanished.

The sagani roared silently and expanded to fill every part of his body. The knight's sword, once almost invisible with speed, slowed. Thoughts fled, replaced by a calm awareness.

The knight attacked, but Tomas saw the cuts coming. He could predict where they would be. Though the knight's control had improved, Tomas saw he used his excessive speed to compensate for a lack of finesse.

There were openings.

Countering the knight's techniques became a simple exercise. Tomas exploited the mistakes, his own sword drawing blood against his younger opponent. He stopped giving up ground and began taking it, driving the knight back, one step at a time.

The knight retreated several steps from a powerful lunge.

Tomas didn't pursue.

The knight flexed every muscle in his body and roared at the sky. Then he looked down at Tomas. The madness seemed to have faded a bit, like a tide leaving behind a sandy beach worn smooth. His voice was even, a brief window of control asserted. "I didn't abandon my soul and sentence myself to the hells to let you win this town," he said.

The knight advanced, his step even, his sword more deadly than ever.

They met again. This duel lacked the unrestrained passion of the last exchange, traded instead for a contest of skill.

Experience made the difference. The openings were smaller and protected more quickly, but they remained. The knight still hadn't fully grown into his new strength. And Tomas punished him for that.

He remained patient. His surroundings had faded, his focus entirely on the duel before him. With Elzeth in every cell in his body, he was beyond anger, beyond impatience. He struck against the openings, forcing the knight commander to work harder and harder to protect himself.

In time, the opportunity he'd been waiting for appeared. He entered it and delivered the fatal blow.

No elation rose in him at the victory.

The women needed his help.

He looked and saw Aron now within ten paces. The assassin had brought his sword up and was preparing to make the killing blow.

Tomas ran, but a small voice in the back of his mind, the one he recognized as his own, knew it was hopeless. The fight with the knight had gone on too long. Tomas had waited too long to unify with Elzeth, his fear dooming his friends. Even now, as fast as he was, he wouldn't reach them in time.

Just as Elzeth's control prevented the rise of joy, though, it also prevented despair. There was only the task.

So he sprinted at Aron, forcing himself to watch as the assassin took aim at Inaya with his sword.

38

J ust as Aron reached Inaya, he suddenly spun
around as though an invisible giant had given him a
friendly punch in the side. Less than a second later,
Tomas heard the crack of a rifle. As Aron spun,
Franz came out from behind the corner of a building,
working the lever action of a rifle and preparing a second
shot.

He moved far too slowly to be successful.

But if nothing else, he'd attracted Aron's attention.
Unfortunately, it was the sort of attention that ended with a
cut across one's neck, or a knife embedded deep within
one's heart. Not the sort of attention an older innkeeper was
looking for.

Franz didn't panic. He worked the lever action smoothly,
though Tomas was sure the innkeeper had never held a rifle
before in his life. He brought the weapon back to his
shoulder.

Franz fired.

But without surprise on his side, he had no chance.

Tomas could see the old man's finger tighten on the trigger from fifty feet away. Aron could certainly see it from ten.

The assassin slid to the side. Franz couldn't react quickly enough, and the bullet passed harmlessly by.

Aron either wasn't aware of Tomas behind him or he didn't care. He gestured toward Franz. "One more shot, old man." He opened his arms wide, providing the target. "Hit me and you can save your family."

Franz chambered another shell and brought the rifle back up. He didn't hurry, and the tip of the rifle was steady. He pulled the trigger.

To no avail.

Aron dodged at just the right time, the bullet once again harmlessly passing by his side. Franz's human reflexes weren't fast enough to keep his aim true.

Franz might not have killed Aron, but he'd bought enough time with his actions for Tomas to reach the fight.

Aron turned to face him and frowned. He looked down the street past Tomas. "You killed the knight?" He spat on the ground. "I was looking forward to that."

Tomas' attention was on the assassin's posture. Franz's first shot had hit Aron's side, ripping through the left edge of his chest. A few inches right and the shot would have been fatal. With Aron burning as hot as he was, the wound was probably already healing. It wasn't enough to slow him down much.

But perhaps enough.

Elzeth and Tomas roared together, and Tomas attacked.

Tomas felt as though a storm of light raged within him. Elzeth raced to every corner of his body at once, strengthening everything from his toes to his sense of smell. His cuts, strong enough to slice through buildings, sought Aron's life.

A grin of mad joy spread across Aron's face as he responded. He had to realize what Tomas had done.

Tomas felt as though flames could emerge from his skin at any time. Elzeth's power and energy were overwhelming.

And intoxicating.

With this strength and speed, he felt invincible. He felt immortal.

And he never wanted to let it go.

The two hosts cut at one another, feet shuffling and sliding in the dust of the street as they struggled to gain the upper hand. If Aron was slowed at all by his wound, he didn't show it.

They broke apart.

Despite Tomas' sacrifice, Aron still had the edge in speed. It was razor thin, but given enough time, that was all that was needed.

A memory arose, unbidden.

One of Elzeth's.

Of him, padding across treetops, leaping silently from branch to branch, his prey below him.

Tomas attacked.

Before their swords met again he leaped, rotating his body so that his feet were over his head. Upside down, he cut at Aron.

Surprised by the unusual angle of attack, Aron stepped back, but he met the cut.

The impact sent Tomas spinning through the air. He hit the ground rolling, then made it to his feet staring at the wall of Jons' gambling hall. He ran a few steps up it, then twisted and dove at Aron from height.

Again, Aron's technique wasn't prepared for such angles. Aron blocked, but the two of them went down in a tangle of limbs and swords.

Tomas felt the blade pierce his stomach.

Not Aron's sword, but another weapon.

Aron pushed off him and they both stood. Tomas looked down and saw a dagger embedded near his navel.

It wasn't fatal. Not with Elzeth. But it would slow him down, and that would mark the end of the duel. He couldn't afford to lose an iota of speed.

Elzeth's roar was that of a wounded beast. Despite the injury, Tomas felt stronger than ever.

Aron tried to step away. But Tomas didn't let him. He pursued.

The battle was lost. The dagger allowed for no other outcome.

But Tomas had promised himself he would keep Franz's family safe.

So he advanced relentlessly. He scored cuts against Aron, who was off balance and on the retreat. But Tomas was hardly winning. For every cut he inflicted on Aron, two appeared on his own body, deeper and closer to vital organs.

Aron only had one disadvantage.

He was still trying to survive the duel.

Eventually, Tomas ran out of options. He allowed an opening, as wide as the thoroughfare they were fighting on, one too good for any trained warrior to pass on.

Aron instinctively took it, stabbing out with his sword into Tomas' stomach. The sword went in next to his dagger, carving out an even deeper chasm in Tomas' organs.

But it provided Tomas just the opening he was searching for. An opening of his own to strike for.

He made the cut, aiming for Aron's neck, ignoring the pain of the steel in his gut. Soon, it wouldn't matter anyway.

His moment of triumph faded almost as soon as it appeared. Aron stepped closer, driving his sword through

Tomas all the way to the guard. Then he was close enough to grab Tomas' wrist and stop the fatal cut. "Nice try," he snarled.

Tomas groaned as his vision swam.

But Elzeth wasn't out of the battle yet. He still churned within Tomas, focusing his attention, giving him strength.

Both of Aron's hands were occupied. Tomas' left hand was over Aron's right, fighting over the embedded sword. And Aron's left was preventing Tomas from cutting off his head.

Tomas let his left hand slip from Aron's right, hoping that it felt like a slip and not an intentional movement.

When Aron didn't react, Tomas smiled.

His left hand gripped the closest weapon, which just happened to be the dagger in his stomach.

"Go to hell," he said.

Assisted by Elzeth, the movement as quick as a lightning strike, he pulled the dagger from his stomach and drove it up under Aron's chin and into his brain. It was only stopped by the top of Aron's skull.

The assassin's eyes went blank and he stumbled backward. Then he fell limply to the ground.

Tomas dropped to his knees. With the final blow, Elzeth had vanished. Tomas didn't know why. He looked down at the sword in his stomach. He gripped it with his bloody hands and pulled. Sharp stabs of burning needles shot through his torso, but he kept pulling.

When the tip of the sword came out, he looked at it for a moment, then collapsed to his side.

He closed his eyes and couldn't find the strength to open them again.

39

Tomas was lost in a place between dreams and reality. Pain spread through his body like a disease, eating him from the inside. He went from shivering to sweating and back again in the blink of an eye.

And he couldn't feel Elzeth.

Or perhaps, in his rare seconds of clarity, he couldn't feel the separation between them anymore.

Memories mixed together like paints splashed against a canvas, so many as to be nearly unrecognizable. Hunting through the ironwood forests. Hiding for a season in the high caves of the Lowtsen Mountains. Pulled in different directions by forces that allowed for no explanations.

There were moments of lucidity as well. He was in a cart, being ferried somewhere he couldn't guess. Kind voices, speaking softly, the words unintelligible. Sometimes he was covered with a blanket. Other times, a cold cloth was pressed against his forehead.

Pillows and soft blankets surrounded him whenever reality interrupted his dreams, but they did little to ease his pain. Every slight shift in the cart sent a fresh needle of pain somewhere new.

In those moments he just wanted to die.

He was ready to die.

But the end wouldn't come.

The memories would return and the pain would fade, but only for a time.

He came to, once, with startling clarity. He had been propped up against some pillows, but the cart was still moving. Inaya sat next to him. "Where are we?" he managed to croak.

"To get you healed," she said.

He nodded, though she hadn't answered his question.

And then a single dream took him, more vivid than all the rest.

He was hungry and tired. Something had been hunting him for days, one of the white-clad two-legs who were swarming this area. She was particularly clever and more persistent than most, pursuing him for the better part of a day. He had the arrows in his side to prove it. Soon, the hunt would be over. But for now, he ran.

He caught the scent of a different two-legs too late. The creature crouched in the cover of a bush, and its sword flashed out as he swiped. Both sword and claw struck true, and both drew blood.

This two-legs did not wear white. It appeared as one of those who often roamed out in front of larger groups of two-legs. That also explained how it had been able to hide for so long.

He roared, and flame burst from him, melting the nearby snow. He attacked, slashing with his claws and driving the two-legs back. Though the creature was strong, it couldn't fight him, not angered like this. Claws scored deep wounds across its chest, arms, and face.

But as it began to die, it stabbed out at him, and its cut struck deep.

They lay there, side by side, their blood pooling and mixing together.

In that mixing, he heard a call.

A welcome.

Some of his kind had joined the two-legs before. He knew it could be done.

Apart, they would die.

He pulled himself forward and met the eye of the two-legs. They stared at each other, and on a level deeper than language, it understood. It moved its head, and he knew it agreed.

He released his physical form, allowing his essence to seek that of the man.

When they met, no pain could compare.

Tomas awoke to strong hands on his shoulders. He opened his eyes and saw Franz on his left and Inaya on his right.

The cart had stopped.

When he stopped flailing they released him.

"Nightmares?" Franz asked.

"Memories," he answered, his voice ragged and harsh to his ears. "Where are we?"

Franz gestured and Tomas looked around. A small rise surrounded them and they were among a grove of trees.

They were at the nexus.

He groaned, knowing what the well-intentioned family had believed.

Franz said, "Inaya remembered you saying the nexus healed you quickly. We felt it was the only way to save you."

Tomas nodded, the pain from the gesture almost enough to make him vomit. He let his eyes travel to his stomach, where blood continued to seep out through the bandages. Though he couldn't feel Elzeth, the sagani had to be keeping him alive.

Otherwise, he should have died long ago.

He was grateful to Franz and his family. He didn't bother to tell them that if he touched the nexus again it was very likely he would die.

Elzeth remained silent and still within him.

"Are you there?" Tomas asked.

His question stirred the smallest flicker of life into Elzeth, but nothing else.

He didn't know if a sagani could die within a host, but if Elzeth died, so did he. Their destinies had been linked together since that fateful day when they'd both made a choice neither of them had fully understood.

Tomas shifted into a straighter sitting position, biting back a cry of agony as the pain threatened to overwhelm him. He saw the clear pool only a few feet away.

They were dying.

If nothing else, he could give Elzeth a chance at life.

"Help me down to the pond," he said.

He blacked out as they moved him, only coming to when his feet touched the warm water.

All three of them were clustered around him, as though their presence might somehow keep his heart beating. He gestured to a rock about as big as his head jutting most of the way out of the grass nearby. "Bring that here."

It was getting harder to speak. Darkness encroached on the edges of his vision again.

Just one more task.

Inaya hefted the rock close.

"Thank you for every—" Franz began.

"Quiet," Tomas said. "No thanks. Listen." He waited until he was sure they were. "Run, and be safe. I might not come up. And that's fine. Just run."

He started taking deep breaths, fighting against the nausea that threatened to overwhelm him. The others watched, and when Tomas felt ready he looked at them all one last time. He hoped he could carry the memory of their faces into whatever hell awaited his soul.

Then he gestured to the rock, which they placed in his hands.

He let himself slip from the edge and drop into the clear pool of the nexus.

The weight of the rock pulled him down, saving him the energy of trying to dive to the depth of the hole in the bedrock. He reached the hole quickly and let go of the rock.

Gently, he swam to the hole, unable to do much more than kick weakly. He didn't need to save any air for the return journey, so he didn't regret his inability to rush.

Once again the blue glow of the stone became visible. Tomas kicked for it, reaching out with his hand.

His fingers brushed against the stone and immediately stuck.

As before, it was as if a crashing wave of energy filled every corner of his body. Elzeth roared back to life.

It was like unity, but so much stronger.

His thoughts returned, no longer muddled by pain or lack of energy.

This *was* unity.

But not with Elzeth, with something much deeper and wider.

Tomas relaxed and allowed the energy to flow freely.

Elzeth, too, seemed more comfortable around the nexus

this time. Or perhaps he was just too tired even with the flow of energy. He didn't fight or struggle. If anything, he seemed curious.

Tomas held his breath and waited for whatever was to come.

His body was warm and the pain had finally gone away.

He thought of Franz and his family, and he was satisfied.

"You did this?" Elzeth asked.

"Blame Franz. Fool brought us all the way out here, thinking he could save us. But I figured there's no point in us both dying here. Go on."

Elzeth didn't move.

"I can't hold my breath forever, friend." And it was true; the blackness at the edges of his vision was becoming familiar, and his world was clearly darkening.

"We saved each other on that mountain."

"After nearly killing each other."

"Still." Elzeth made no move.

Tomas waited. Soon, he would need to breathe again. But Elzeth seemed to be in no rush.

"It's been an honor to be your host, Elzeth." Tomas closed his eyes and waited for his last breath.

Time lost meaning, and although his rational mind knew it hadn't been more than a second or two, it felt like an eternity. He didn't feel Elzeth moving at all, despite the energy washing through his body.

Then Elzeth stirred, his presence unifying with Tomas' once again.

When the sagani spoke, his voice was soft, but determined all the same.

"No. Not like this."

EPILOGUE

Tomas sat at the edge of the pond, letting the last of his clothes dry off in the sun. Elissa had done her best to patch and clean them, but there were so many holes and so much blood it was a pointless task. If he ever came across another town, he'd have to buy himself new ones.

But he had a feeling he'd be avoiding towns for some time.

For decency's sake he'd thrown a blanket over his shoulders, and the warmth of the day was making him drowsy.

Inaya and Elissa sat apart from him, basking in the warmth of the sun and the surprising joy of not having anything to do.

Tomas heard Franz before the others, and soon enough he was cresting the rise on one of the newly acquired horses. He rode to his family and Tomas stood up and walked over to join them.

He felt good.

Better than good, actually.

He felt the best he'd ever felt.

Once they were together, Franz gave them the news.

"Town's as good as gone," he said. "A few homes might be repaired, but don't see why they would. Most travelers choose the southern route, and with both the church and the Family gone, no reason for anyone to settle there anymore."

Tomas wondered if Franz was right.

Perhaps for a time. But eventually, people would come again. The nexus practically guaranteed it.

Tomas planned on being well away by the time that came to pass.

The family took the news of the loss of the town with surprising aplomb. The inn had been all they cared about, and they'd had a few days to adjust to that loss. The town hadn't meant much more to them.

That night, Franz prepared one last meal for them all. They ate, and the food was as delicious as anything Tomas had ever tasted.

Inaya and Elissa went to bed early that night, but Franz and Tomas climbed to the top of the rise to stare at the stars.

"You know you're welcome among us. I'm sure you've noticed Inaya has taken a fancy to you."

"As good a reason as any to leave. She'll not find the happiness she seeks with me."

Franz snorted. "You're wiser than you look. I would have given my blessing, though, on account of all you've done. And I believe you'd treat her well."

Tomas laughed. "Have no fear on that account. Tomorrow we part."

"You sure you won't at least join us on our way to Tansai?"

Tomas shook his head. "With all the family in town dead, there's no one left to hunt you. The rifles will keep you safe from any wildlife who wander too close. No one besides us knows what you did. You'll be safe. And Tansai is the wrong direction."

"You're still decided?"

"Can't say this whole incident convinced me any different. Further I can stay from most people, better off I think we'll all be."

"I wish there was a way to repay you for what you've done for us."

Tomas shook his head. "You saved my life twice. If anything, I owe you."

Franz extended his hand. "Call it even?"

Tomas took it and shook it firmly. "Even it is."

They watched the stars in silence for a long time then, only going to bed once Shen had joined Tolkin in the sky.

THE NEXT MORNING dawned clear with just a hint of a bite in the air. Autumn was a ways off yet, but it was coming. Tomas woke late to the sounds of Franz and the others packing up.

Tomas watched them, keeping his distance.

Franz had lost his inn, but was walking away from town richer than he would have believed possible a few days ago. They'd taken both the enormous smuggling cart and the draft horses from the Family stables. Elissa had also had the presence of mind to rob Jons' gambling hall of everything she could, including a few choice bottles. Tomas had taken just one as his own recompense.

In a fair world, the amount they'd stolen from the Family wasn't even near what the inn should have been worth. But considering the inn was failing and no one but the church or Family would have purchased the property, the loot was a bit of a windfall for Franz and his family.

Once they returned to Tansai and sold the horses, cart, rifles, and more, they'd have enough coin to do whatever they wished.

He knew they'd talked of their plans with one another, but he hadn't inquired. They were safe and that was all that mattered. He wouldn't see them again, anyhow.

Tomas packed up his own gear, light as it was. Franz had offered to share more of the loot, but Tomas had all he needed.

They met one last time by the side of the pond. Franz got to his knees first, then bowed his head all the way to the grass. Inaya and Elissa followed suit.

They were adherents of the old ways, all the way to the end.

Tomas bowed deeply to them, and it didn't seem like there were enough words to wish them all the good fortune he hoped they experienced back east.

The family piled into the cart and Inaya urged the horses into motion. Tomas stopped on the rise surrounding the nexus and watched them go, returning their farewell waves. He watched for a while, until they were a small smudge in the endless prairie.

Then he walked away.

HE'D FOUND A GAME TRAIL, thin but well-worn from the deer in the area. The scat nearby was practically a traveler's log of the animals that made use of the path.

Elzeth hadn't stirred much since the nexus. Tomas had given the sagani space, knowing it was what was desired. But now they were alone once again, with nothing but miles of grassland to pass the time. "You want to talk?"

"Only if the company is better than what I'm used to."

Tomas smiled at the snide remark. "I haven't said 'thank you.'"

"No, you haven't."

"Thank you. I didn't even think I could be saved."

"Well, I healed your body, but your soul was too shriveled to do anything about."

Tomas laughed out loud. He felt good.

Elzeth turned serious. "The power available at that nexus was something else, though. With it, I was able to do more than I ever believed possible. Are you sure it's wise for us to leave it?"

"Not much we could do, one way or another. Both the Family and the church knows it's there. They'll come after it again, eventually. Don't like leaving it, but there's nothing I could have done about it anyhow, not in any meaningful way."

Tomas walked for a while before working up the courage to ask the question that had really been bothering him. "Why?"

He felt Elzeth stirring, about to give another sarcastic rebuttal, but the sagani changed its mind. "I wasn't ready for this to be over."

A lump formed in Tomas' throat, which he swallowed down with effort. "I would have missed you, too."

Elzeth didn't respond at first, but Tomas felt the tension building within him. "No, you wouldn't have. You'd have been dead."

Tomas chuckled. "True enough." He stopped walking. "Together, then?"

"Together."

A hundred paces later, Tomas came to a fork in the path. One trail looked like it tracked further north while the other went pretty much west.

"You're not going to throw another stick in the air, are you?" Elzeth asked.

Tomas shook his head. "No. That, it turns out, didn't end well. West?"

"West."

THE ADVENTURES CONTINUE!

Top o' the morning!

I hope that wherever you are in the world, and whenever it is you're reading this, that you're doing well.

First, as an author, let me thank you for reading *Last Sword in the West*. Whether this is the first book of mine you've read or my twentieth, I hope that you enjoyed it. There have never been more ways to be entertained, and it truly means the world to me that you choose to spend your time in these pages.

If you enjoyed the story, rest assured the Tomas' and Elzeth's next adventure is right around the corner. *Eyes of the Hidden World* continues their wanderings, and you can order it now, wherever books are sold.

And if you're looking to spread the word, there's few better ways to support the story by leaving a review where you purchased the book!

STAY IN TOUCH

Thanks once again for reading *Last Sword in the West*. I had a tremendous amount of fun writing this story, and am looking forward to writing more of Tomas and Elzeth.

If you enjoyed the story, I'd ask that you consider signing up to get emails from me. You can do so at:

www.waterstonemedia.net/newsletter

I typically email readers once or twice a month, and one of my greatest pleasures over the past five years has been getting to know the people reading my stories.

If I'm being honest, email is my favorite way of communicating with readers. Whether it's hearing from soldiers stationed overseas or grandmothers tending to their gardens, email has allowed me to make new friends all over the world.

Email subscribers also get all the goodies. From free books in all formats, to sample chapters and surprise short stories, if I'm giving something away, it's through email.

I hope you'll join us.

Ryan

ALSO BY RYAN KIRK

Last Sword in the West

Last Sword in the West

Eyes of the Hidden World

Relentless

Relentless Souls

Heart of Defiance

Their Spirit Unbroken

Oblivion's Gate

The Gate Beyond Oblivion

The Gates of Memory

The Gate to Redemption

The Nightblade Series

Nightblade

World's Edge

The Wind and the Void

Blades of the Fallen

Nightblade's Vengeance

Nightblade's Honor

Nightblade's End

The Primal Series

Primal Dawn

Primal Darkness
Primal Destiny
Primal Trilogy

ABOUT THE AUTHOR

Ryan Kirk is the bestselling author of the *Nightblade* series of books. When he isn't writing, you can probably find him playing disc golf or hiking through the woods.

www.ryankirkauthor.com
www.waterstonemedia.net
contact@waterstonemedia.net

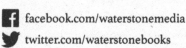 facebook.com/waterstonemedia
twitter.com/waterstonebooks
 instagram.com/waterstonebooks

CPSIA information can be obtained
at www.ICGtesting.com
Printed in the USA
LVHW041335311021
702031LV00016B/693